TUNNEL RATS

MUD AND BLOOD

CLIFF BANKS

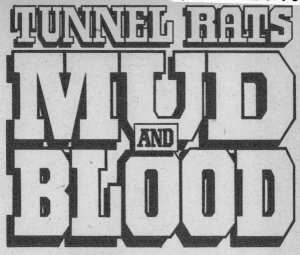

POPULAR LIBRARY

An Imprint of Warner Books, Inc.

A Warner Communications Company

ONE

Dawn.

The jungle sweltered.

The four-man patrol moved silently at combat intervals along the winding, narrow game trail.

Lieutenant Scott Gaines, the second man in the line, drew his sleeve across his face to wipe the sweat from his eyes without releasing the two-handed grip on his M-16.

Like the men of his squad, he traveled light: besides the rifle, his only gear consisted of a canteen and a flashlight clipped to the ammo belt worn around his waist, and a small pouch and extra ammunition, also clipped to the belt.

DeLuca moved at a steady clip behind him. Hidalgo brought up the rear. The point man was Bok Van Tu, the team's Kit Carson scout.

The depths of the jungle were still shrouded in a gloomy, humid half-light, the first rays of daylight barely penetrating the overhead canopy of joined branches, vines, and leaves of the palm, balsa, mahogany, and eucalyptus trees that hemmed the trail in as if trying to smother it.

The vegetation on all sides stunk of decay and crackled with the cacophonous symphony of birds, insects, and monkeys.

Up ahead, Tu came to a stop. Without turning back he made a motion for the others to join him.

They reached his side to group at a point where the hilly terrain flattened for a stretch, the trail widening where the rays of sunlight had not yet topped the surrounding trees to dissipate the mist.

Tu pointed across the clearing. "There," he whispered.

Gaines had to work to focus his eyes for several seconds before he discerned what the scout was pointing at through the mist.

A man in the black pajama "uniform" of the Vietcong squatted with his back against the vine-covered trunk of a tree. The man idly smoked a cigarette. An AK-47 assault rifle was propped up next to him, leaning against the tree. The man slapped irritably at a mosquito at the back of his neck, drew his palm away, and looked at it, wholly unaware of the presence of those who spied upon him.

DeLuca and Hidalgo saw the man but kept their rifles and eyes panning the clearing and their backtrack along the trail for any sign of trouble.

"All right, I'll take that one," Gaines whispered. "There are supposed to be two more."

"Mathematically, it couldn't be improved upon," De-Luca grunted.

Hidalgo nodded. "Real obliging of the bastards."

"Can the chatter," Gaines warned. He tapped Hidalgo and pointed off to their left along the treeline. "Johnny, see what you find over that way." He pointed in the opposite direction for DeLuca. "Sergeant, your man should be over there, not far. Tu, you know the signal if you hear anyone coming up on us. Rendezvous back here ASAP. Okay, let's do it."

They faded away, disappearing from each other's sight into the wall of green that was the dense, hilly jungle.

Gaines's last sight of Tu was of the scout crouching behind a tree trunk at the edge of the trail, his rifle slung over his shoulder, his machete drawn.

Gaines took longer than he would have liked to circle around on the sentry across the clearing, but within five paces of leaving the others, he spotted a trip wire strung at ankle height between two tree trunks.

He stepped back and used the barrel of his rifle to pop the wire, and without a sound a hardened ball of clay, sprouting countless sharpened bamboo splinters, sliced through the air where his head would have been if his boot had tripped the wire.

The device whacked harmlessly into a tree trunk.

Gaines continued on, staying just inside the treeline, taking time to watch for more trip wires but finding none.

When he reached a point five feet behind the sentry squatting at the base of the tree, Gaines reached into the pouch clipped to his ammo belt and withdrew the wire garrote, then threw himself at the man, looping the garrote around the man's throat.

It was a by-the-numbers kill. While tightening the garrote and twisting it murderously from behind, Gaines dragged the struggling figure back out of sight into the brush. He flung the man to the ground, facedown, and knelt a knee into the base of the sentry's spine.

The sentry gasped and grunted and struggled, but the damp jungle floor muffled the death sounds.

When the gasping and struggling stopped, Gaines

snapped the man's neck with a brutal, two-handed twist just to make sure he was dead.

Gaines reclaimed the garrote from around the dead man's throat and returned it to the pouch. He unslung the M-16, returned it to a two-handed firing position, and commenced working his way back to regroup with the others, again using extreme care to watch where he stepped.

The jungle appeared unchanged, uninhabited, all around him. The whistling, chirping animal sounds continued unabated. The temperature continued to climb with every passing minute.

One could not tell that a battalion of Vietcong were positioned less than twenty feet away . . . *underground*.

Gaines and his men were part of a highly classified special forces operation with the Intelligence and Reconnaisance Section of the 1st Engineer Battalion of the 1st U.S. Infantry Division, the Big Red One.

Gaines's team had been the first of several squads that became known as the Tunnel Rats, the Army's answer to the threat posed by the VC's use of more than two hundred miles of secret tunnel networks located around Saigon. In the damp black holes, designed for slim Vietnamese, most Americans found only claustrophobic panic.

The Tunnel Rats had managed very quickly to attain near-legendary status in American and enemy ranks, for theirs was a war fought not aboveground with standard military hardware, strategies, and technology, but beneath, where they took on the enemy on his own turf, one on one, and where the only things that decided who lived and who died were guts, strength, and skill.

Gaines's team was on fifteen-minute standby at the base at Lai Kai, although a bit more planning and prep had gone into this mission than they were used to.

The Rats' status derived from their ability to execute extremely stressful and unnatural tasks in the course of their regular duties, which in their case meant crawling through narrow, totally dark, low earthen tunnels, taking on the heavily armed VC units hiding out there. Gaines's team had scored the highest ratio of mission successes since the inception of the Tunnel Rats operation.

Gaines was twenty-five years old, lean but well muscled. He was ideally suited to helping to devise and lead such a team. Born and raised in Butte, Montana, he was the son of a mining engineer and had spent much of his youth and young manhood exploring the abandoned mine shafts in and around his hometown. He had later dropped out of Montana Tech, the School of Mines, to work full-time with his father, becoming an explosives expert.

Gaines was a draftee who had gone on to graduate from officer candidate school. He had seen more than his share of fighting since becoming a Tunnel Rat, mostly in the northern provinces, where he had earned a Silver Star, a Bronze Star, and the Army Commendation Medal during his double tour of combat duty.

He reached the point where the game trail met the clearing at the treeline. DeLuca and Hidalgo joined him from the directions they had taken, and Tu emerged from his position behind the tree trunk.

"Find your men?" Gaines asked.

"Found him and greased him," said DeLuca.

"Ditto," said Hidalgo.

Like Gaines, the American grunts of his team were physically well suited to the particular demands of Tunnel Rat fighting.

Sergeant (E-5) Frank DeLuca, age twenty-one, black-haired, muscular, and fiery, had been an amateur featherweight in the tough Roxbury section of Boston before his local draft board had sent him greetings.

PFC Johnny Hidalgo, nineteen, had spent his civilian life hustling for survival on the mean streets of the east L.A. barrio. He was short, wiry, but every inch of him was rock solid.

This mission was different than most.

This was an area ruled by the VC after the sun went down, no matter what the press releases from the headshed in Saigon said to the contrary.

An infantry battalion from the 1st had been deployed in an air-mobile insertion the night before. There had been a firefight in the vicinity, and charlie had vanished as he always did, or seemed to.

The break this time around had come from a captured VC who sang like a canary once the interrogators got him off to the side. What he had to say had brought Gaines and his team to the office of Captain Harrison Carter, the Battalion S-2, or intelligence officer: Carter was the Rat Six, the Division's code word for commander, and it was he who handed the Tunnel Rats their assignments.

"If our information is correct, and I'm inclined to believe it is," Carter had told them, "then we've pinpointed the operation center headquarters for the entire VC military region. We are talking battalion strength, and the sweet thing is, they probably don't know that we know. The troops on the ground have been pulled back. We showed our prisoner a topo map, and he's been very cooperative, pinpointed the entrances and placed the guards."

"Unless the punk has a sense of humor," DeLuca said, "and is getting ready to laugh his ass off when we walk into a friggin' ambush."

"If that happens, he won't have an ass to laugh off, and he knows it," Carter said grimly.

"My informants have told me of an underground headquarters in that region," said Tu. "I myself have heard mention of it, but Captain Quang, who commands the VC battalion of this region, is known for his secrecy. I have heard the operations center relocates regularly to different tunnels."

Bok Van Tu was thirty-eight years old. His compact physique was sturdy. The deep furrows grooved into his narrow, leathery face bespoke a lifetime of hardship. His mouth flashed yellowed teeth, some missing. His eyes glittered with a lively intelligence.

Tu knew the tunnels better than anyone on the team. The only one of his company to survive a firefight with a squad of marines several years before, he had defected from the Cong to save himself, his wife, and three children from the relentless American offensive.

His skills included familiarity with local dialects and an intimate firsthand knowledge of VC tactics and tunnel layout. He was committed wholeheartedly to the ideal of a free democratic government for Vietnam.

In the early days, when Gaines's Tunnel Rats team were learning to work together and getting to know each other some, DeLuca especially, had questioned Tu's loyalties.

Such suspicions, however, had been long ago put to rest. Tu was a fully equal member of the team and had proven himself to be a strong asset countless times both for his sources of information and for the insight he provided into the Vietnamese perspective on things, something Gaines found essential in a war like this, submerged as the Americans were in a wholly alien culture and environment.

"Quang and his men will be down there tomorrow," Carter had said. "About one hundred strong, thinking they're safe and sound while our forces comb the whole region right above them without finding a thing. Only this time, we have found them and they don't know that we know."

"Even if they suspect we know they're down there," said Gaines, "they won't have time to relocate if we move fast enough. They'll stay put during the daylight hours if we have a sizable force in the area."

"Which we do," said Carter. "As I said, I've ordered the troops to stay clear of the tunnels. I don't want to tip our hand to Quang and his force. You'll have plenty of backup if you need it, and there'll be a net around the area to catch any VC you flush out . . . if any do make it out," he added pointedly. "But this is the kind of job you men have been trained for, and if the feather touch you guys have got doesn't get it, a lot of good men are going to buy it in that jungle when Quang does get wind that we know he's down there and that battalion of his decides to try to blast their way out."

"So what are we waiting for?" Hidalgo had asked with that cocky, always-ready-for-action grin of his.

"Not a damn thing, now." Carter had rolled up the topographic map and handed it to Gaines. "Something for you to look over on the chopper. You'll be dropped in about half a klick from the main tunnel entrance. You should reach the site right about dawn."

And they had been on their way. . . .

Right on schedule, thought Gaines as he scanned the clearing before them, searching one more time for any indication of activity and finding none.

The choppers had not touched down. Gaines and his men had rappelled down ropes and advanced along the trail that wended its way through the thick jungle, from a direction where Quang's aboveground sentries had least expected an attack, the last miscalculation of their lives.

"Looks all clear," Gaines whispered to his men. "Careful, now."

He left the treeline. His men started across the clearing with him, toward the concealed main tunnel entrance. The team spread out.

They had not gone ten feet from the treeline when Tu came to a stop and motioned for them to stop, his expression deadly serious as he cocked his head, listening keenly.

"I heard something," he whispered.

Gaines hadn't heard a thing, but he drew up short, swiveling around, as did DeLuca and Hidalgo.

"Are you sure?"

Tu bent quickly to the ground, kneeling, placing his ear to the path of the game trail.

"Several men, moving quickly," he said. "A patrol. Not Americans. Not boots. Sandals."

"So the VC don't move around this tunnel in the daylight, huh?" DeLuca grunted.

"Someone forgot to tell the VC that." Hidalgo chuckled with enthusiasm, the way he always did when action was on the way.

"Take cover," said Gaines. "When they show, take 'em down. If they find the sentries dead, they'll sound the alarm."

This was not meant to be a flush action. Often the Rats were assigned to go into hot holes with the intention of smoking out the guerrillas, forcing them backwards out of a complex's escape holes for the aboveground force to capture or pick off.

Not this time.

There was too much at stake. This hit called for the feather touch, as Carter had said, precision timing, and a whole load of luck.

Even Gaines's Tunnel Rats could not take on the battalion-strength enemy force that would pour out of that tunnel to investigate or defend if an alarm was sounded.

And Gaines had learned long ago to place full faith in Tu's near sixth-sense knowledge of these jungles. Tu was of the jungle. He knew and understood them as no foreigner, certainly no Westerner, could ever hope to.

They had almost gained the treeline again when the point man of the returning patrol emerged from the game trail: a kid of no more than fifteen or sixteen, clad in black pajamas, his figure dwarfed by the AK-47 he carried at port arms, trotted into view. His eyes popped and his jaw dropped when he saw Tu and the Americans, and that was all he had time for.

Gaines was nearest the kid, about ten feet away. He unsheathed his knife, flung it with deadly accuracy in one lightning movement.

The blade buried itself to the handle in the young Vietcong's heart region. The kid grabbed at it with both hands, then his knees knocked and he collapsed and did not move. By that time Gaines was running past, barely slowing to pluck the knife from the dead boy's chest on his way toward the cover already gained by his men.

The five men of the patrol, dressed and armed like the dead boy, appeared seconds later. The next man along almost tripped over the kid's body and then the five of them were bunching together to look down at it, careless because they were so close to their base and because they were gripped by surprise.

"Take 'em!" Gaines snarled.

The Tunnel Rats flung themselves from their cover along both sides of the trail, lunging at the VC.

TWO

The five VC didn't stand a chance, did not even have time enough to react except for startled shouts and gasps as death swooped down on them.

Hidalgo, DeLuca, and Tu each flung himself upon one of the VC, each tumbling his man to the ground.

Slashing knives flashed in the sunlight. Gurgling death rattles burbled beneath the thrashing sounds of violent death.

Gaines took his man out, then whirled to find the last unfortunate of the patrol.

This one had just enough reaction time to backpedal several paces and track his rifle toward Gaines.

Gaines was about to fling his knife to take out the man as he had the point man, but before he could, Hidalgo came up on the VC from behind, snaked a forearm around the VC's throat, and jerked him back sharply. Hidalgo rammed his knife in a couple of times, steadying the VC, who stood up on his tiptoes and emitted the strangest sort of wheezing sound as he died.

It was over in less than thirty seconds.

Gaines and the three men of his team moved as one with the crack precision of a killing machine.

"Let's get them out of sight in case somebody else unexpected stumbles along," said Gaines.

The overripe stench of death hung heavy on the humid, motionless air. The Tunnel Rats roughly dragged the corpses deeper into the vegetation along the trail. Flies were already buzzing raucously, drawn to the spilled blood.

"Now that that's out of the way," DeLuca groused as they regrouped, "maybe we can get down to business."

"Yeah." Hidalgo nodded. "Some serious killing."

"Move out." Gaines kept his voice pitched to a low whisper. "This one's got to be like walking on eggs, guys."

They moved out.

The tunnel complex was less than a mile from the Thi Tinh River, which meandered through a valley to the west. Thanks to its proximity to the river, the soil in this region was predominantly laterite clay, ideal for fortification. The roots of the surrounding, towering trees strengthened the tunnels the way reinforced concrete would strengthen an aboveground structure.

At a spot near where Gaines had killed the sentry, he motioned to his men to start looking. He and DeLuca and Hidalgo commenced scrutinizing the ground minutely, inch by inch, knowing exactly what they were looking for.

Tu stood with his finger around the M-16's trigger as he turned in slow circles, his keen, squinting eyes scanning the jungle countryside surrounding their vulnerable position there in the clearing.

If things had gone the way they were supposed to from

the VC commander's point of view, then one or all of the three sentries he had positioned up here would have seen the approach of anyone coming across the clearing toward the tunnel entrance and would have had plenty of time to pick them off. Smart thinking on Quang's part, thought Gaines.

DeLuca found the trapdoor.

It was made of wood, was small—only sixteen by eleven inches—was perforated with air holes, and had beveled sides designed to prevent it from dropping into the tunnel below.

The dead leaves on the ground that concealed the trapdoor were fully brushed away. Hidalgo and DeLuca stood above the trapdoor with their rifles aimed at it, while Gaines bent forward to grasp the rope handle and yank the trapdoor open.

Revealed was a hole about fifteen feet deep. At one side of the bottom, it curved away, forming another shaft.

"Who gets to have the fun?" DeLuca asked.

It was standard procedure that no one ever went into a hole alone, and once inside the tunnels, no one ever wandered more than five yards ahead of the next man.

"You and me, Sarge," said Gaines. "Johnny, you keep Tu company and enjoy the sunshine. Call in the choppers if it gets hairy up here."

"Gotcha." Johnny nodded. He joined Tu in scouting the surrounding terrain, a TR-12 radio strapped to his back.

Gaines and DeLuca set down their rifles, tossed down their jungle fighter's bush hats, and rapidly stripped to the waist.

The Tunnel Rats' equipment when going into a hole seldom varied: flashlight, pistol, knife, and a short length of stick and wire, which the men now getting ready to go down removed from their pouches.

There was one addition this time.

Because of the odds and because they didn't have full-scale backup directly overhead as usual, Gaines had suggested bringing along a bit of extra firepower.

DeLuca wore, strapped across his back, an M-2 carbine with a so-called "paratrooper stock," which folded up, making the weapon no more than twenty-two inches in length, ideal for tunnel work, unlike the much bigger M-16s, which were wholly impractical in the tunnels for the type of work the Rats specialized in.

"I'll take point," Gaines told DeLuca.

DeLuca registered real disappointment. "Aw, Lieutenant—"

"Just keep that cannon ready to pass it forward to me if we run into anyone down there," Gaines said with a nod to the M-2.

Gaines's principal responsibility would be to plant the C-4 explosive he carried wrapped within the pouch clipped to his belt.

When they were ready to go into the hole, Tu handed Hidalgo the length of rope he wore notched to his belt. He resumed sole lookout while Hidalgo lowered first Gaines, then DeLuca into the access shaft using the rope.

Gaines's parting words to Hidalgo, as he lowered himself down the rope, were "Raise our friends on the radio. Let them know the ball's in play."

"Will do," Hidalgo promised.

At the bottom of the hole, Gaines released the rope and, before DeLuca started down, went into a crouch and entered the black depths of the side passage.

The familiar embrace of the tunnels after the steambath heat of the jungle up above felt almost refreshing—until one thought about what lay ahead.

The Cong were known for the fiendish cleverness with

which they bobby-trapped the tunnels specifically in anticipation of the Tunnel Rats.

There were real rats: tethered, bubonic plaque–infected rates. And wired grenades, the trip wires made out of jungle tree roots. Not to mention all the other nasty things that made their home down here: snakes, scorpions, and countless unidentifiable rejects of nature.

Gaines, blinded by the abrupt change from sunlight to total blackness, tied his flashlight to the stick. He held the flash away from his body in case there was someone down at the far end of this tunnel, waiting for something to shoot at, to blow his head off. More than one Tunnel Rat had ended that way.

He flicked on the flash.

The beam probed a tunnel that ran straight for about ten yards, by Gaines's estimation, before bending around to the right. The tunnel was no wider than two and a half feet, no higher than three feet.

These dimensions would be sufficient. Gaines intended to plant the explosive halfway down to that bend in order for the blast to have maximum impact on the vast complex farther below.

He started crawling forward. Earth and rivulets of sweat started to fill his eyes, the ground beneath him stripping away the skin from his knees and elbows.

His body was adjusting to the temperature down here, and his movement generated body heat in the tight confines, making the tunnel seem no longer cool.

There was the chance a VC was sitting right around the curve in the tunnel, that he had seen the beam and would be waiting.

That was the one similarity between combat down in the tunnels and up on the surface, thought Gaines. You never knew when or where the enemy would be lying in wait next, and that made for a tension in the gut that even a long-timer like Gaines could never shake.

He heard DeLuca coming into the tunnel after him.

Gaines reached the spot he felt would be the best place for setting the C-4 and wedged it against the curved floor of the tunnel. Then he unraveled a length of fuse wire and attached it to the clump of high explosives.

When the charge was set, Gaines started scooting backward toward the access hole, unraveling the carefully pre-measured length of fuse wire.

The charge should cave in the whole structure.

DeLuca started easing out into the access hole. Hidalgo dropped the rope down to him. DeLuca grabbed it and started to climb back out. Despite his slight physical stature, Hidalgo stood up there like a marble pillar, his muscles bulging in the sun, supporting DeLuca's weight.

Gaines straightened into a crouch when he eased himself from the tunnel and back into the access hole. The rope dangled next to him.

He lighted the end of the length of fuse. Then he grabbed the rope with both hands, grabbed a footing on one wall of the access hole, and started climbing like hell.

When he emerged from the hole, the sunlight nearly blinded him as much as the darkness below had.

Hidalgo tossed the rope back to Tu, who rewound it and snapped it back to his belt while Gaines and DeLuca quickly donned their shirts, reorganizing themselves. Hidalgo kept turning in tight circles, his rifle up.

"We'd best make tracks," said Gaines moments later.

"I hear that," said Hidalgo. "Man, I haven't even had breakfast yet."

"Always thinking about food," DeLuca chided him.

They angled away from the trapdoor, automatically assuming combat intervals.

Tu suddenly held up his hand for them to stop. He turned to Gaines with a worried expression on his face and started to speak.

In the near distance, from the direction in which they were heading but inside the treeline, came a hollow *whump!* sound that Gaines recognized immediately.

Mortar fire!

"Incoming!" Gaines shouted.

He threw himself to the ground and saw the others do the same. An instant later the blast came, geysering dirt and exploding shrapnel.

Several automatic weapons started chattering at them from the treeline, the distinctive cracking sound of the AK-47s underscoring the spitting whistle sounds of projectiles nipping the air close overhead.

"Shit!" Gaines heard Bok Van Tu say with feeling.

Ngai Quang, Captain of the People's Army of the Socialist Republic of Vietnam, commander of the Vietcong's Seventh Battalion, embraced his oldest son, Tsing, his only surviving son.

Sorrow welled up within Quang. He broke the contact and stepped back, killing the emotions stirring within him.

His wife, his daughter, and his youngest son had been dead for several years now. They had been killed by American bombs during the early days of the war.

The only emotion he had indulged in since the initial grief passed had been hatred for the Americans who had taken nearly everything from him. Everything except Tsing. When he was with his son, he ached. He told himself that this was a good thing, because it meant humanity still lived within him.

Tsing reminded Quang of himself at that age, indignant

and full of anger and outrage that foreign powers would dare think it their right to colonize the land of his birth.

Quang had been busy receiving reports from his squad leaders regarding activities and enemy engagements of the night before, when Tsing, traveling by himself, reached the tunnel complex.

Tsing had eaten a hurried meal of rice compacted into balls, washed down with strong tea. Then he had received word that his father awaited him.

"Did you encounter Lieutenant Pham on your way here?" Quang asked his son.

"I did not, Father. He is missing?"

Quang nodded. "There was a firefight last night. We suffered heavy casualties. Lieutenant Pham was among the missing."

"You think the Americans have him?"

"I hope they do not, but I'm afraid they do."

"I was beginning to worry about Pham."

"I too, my son. Life in the tunnels was wearing down what was once a fine fighter. I see now that he should have been relieved of duty long ago."

"Perhaps his mind snapped," said Tsing, "and he has disappeared on his own. He could take no more of life down here."

"If the Americans have him," said Quang, "then Pham will talk. I have sent out additional security patrols."

"In the daylight? With the Americans practically overhead, Father, do you not think we court disaster if they track the patrols here?"

"It is not important that we detect any enemy presence that may show signs they know we are here," said Quang. "I have already given orders to the men to spend the day preparing to evacuate as soon as the sun falls. But our precautions may already be too late. I do not underestimate the Americans."

"It will depend on Pham, then," said Tsing, "on whether or not he had been made to talk."

They sat upon overturned ammunition crates in a conference chamber, a big room about eight feet high, dimly lighted.

Electrical power in the complex was provided by a Honda motorcycle engine, buried at the lowest level of the complex, from where its noise could not reach the surface.

Ngai Quang and his son, and Pham and many others, had made these tunnels their home for more than five months now.

This complex, like many others in the region, had originally been dug as a hiding place and staging area for the Viet Minh, nationalist guerrillas who had fought the French in the forties and fifties.

The elaborate complex included one other conference center like this one, as well as sleeping chambers, a field hospital, storerooms, a kitchen, an air-raid shelter, a latrine, and a cleaning area.

The complex was self-contained, the storerooms full of cached-away rice donated by sympathetic farmers, in many cases family members of those Quang commanded. The kitchen personnel cooked at night. The smoke was diluted through several channels of air ducts that made it scarcely visible from the ground-level chimneys.

Life in the tunnels was anything but luxurious, and more than one man had broken mentally, like Pham, under the stressful day-to-day conditions.

Quang's small sleeping area, for instance, was no more than seventy centimeters by eighty centimeters and one meter high, and the deeper you were in the tunnel complex, the greater the chance of your being buried alive. It was a fear that could work on the strongest of nerves, Quang knew.

There would be artillery to move, too, he reminded himself. The battalion had, stored away in these tunnels, several 105mm field artillery howitzers that were kept stripped and oiled, ready for quick reassembly and action.

Quang put these thoughts from his mind, concentrating on the matter at hand.

"You were told not to risk coming back here until all was in readiness," he said.

"As it is, or will be very soon," said Tsing. "The tunnel being dug beneath the American base at Lai Khe is all but completed."

Enthusiasm sparkled in the young man's eyes, and another ache of sorrow stabbed at Quang deep inside. Tsing had his mother's eyes.

"I will alert our men positioned inside the ARVN battalion stationed there to be ready," said Quang. "You and your team of diggers have done well, my son."

Tsing accepted this paternal praise with a beaming smile.

"Thank you, my father. We will be inside the Americans' base within twenty-four hours."

Quang was about to say something when a dull, far-away-sounding *thud* from the surface far above worked its way down to their ears.

A moment later a man scampered into the chamber from the access tunnel.

"Trouble, Captain. There is fighting up above!"

"To arms," Quang shouted, leaping to his feet.

"It seems Pham was captured," Tsing said to his father. "What shall we do?" The question was asked calmly but earnestly.

Quang was proud of Tsing's grace under fire, but he knew there was no time to tell him now.

"We must escape and be prepared to fight to the death," he answered in the same calm voice, starting toward the hole to the access tunnel. "Quickly now, if we want to live. There is no time to lose!"

THREE

Gaines estimated two separate points of origin of the heavy automatic fire pinning him and his Rats down in the high elephant grass of the clearing.

Quang must have defied the Vietcong's standard operating procedure and sent more than one daylight patrol out to scout the vicinity, he realized.

Underground, the fuse wire burned, shortening fast toward that massive charge of planted C-4. . . .

The auto fire from the treeline continued unabated. Bullets bit and nipped at the grass as the kids in VC rags readjusted their fire. Before long they would have it right, Gaines knew, and he and his men would be dead.

"Call in those choppers," he said calmly to Hidalgo.

"You got 'em," Hidalgo said, and started barking curtly into the radio he carried. "Big Brother, this is Brother Rat. We need out of here, man, and fast. We're under fire. It's a hot LZ. We need out of here, Big Brother."

"On our way, Brother Rat," the response crackled back with static.

DeLuca loosed a burst from his M-16. "We also need a diversion," he snarled. "How long to the blow, Lieutenant?"

"Any second now," said Gaines. "Let's work our way right down the middle so we have some cover until the choppers get here."

This VC patrol had been split in two by its leader. Gaines could tell from the angles of incoming fire, which were about five hundred yards apart. Probably three Kalashnikovs pouring in fire from each position.

He and his men moved out in low combat crouches. Each man fired as he ran, Hidalgo and Tu blazing away in one direction, DeLuca and Gaines pouring it on the other shooters.

The fire from both positions tapered off into nothing, but there was no way to tell if the VC had been hit. The wall of green that was the treeline was too dense along here to be certain of anything.

They had just made it to the treeline when the charge of C-4 blew.

The massive blast ripped the earth asunder in a geysering, spewing, bursting eruption that filled the air with flying chunks of unsettled dirt and rock.

The powerful force of the explosion lifted the four men off their feet, throwing them forward into the jungle as if swatted by an invisible giant fist, the hot breath of the blast clawing at their backs.

They pulled themselves up into combat crouches while debris was still settling, again facing off with well-trained precision, Hidalgo and Tu pulling their weapons around in the one direction from which they had received fire, Gaines and DeLuca toward the other.

The earth around the tunnel complex was settling into a sinking depression that looked like the beginnings of a giant sinkhole. Gaines could tell the C-4 had done its work.

The fading echoes of the blast gave way to the familiar *whompa-whompa-whompa* of two rapidly approaching Huey gunships.

Again AK-47s commenced stuttering toward the team from the direction faced by Tu and Hidalgo, who immediately returned heavy fire. Projectiles chewed at tree trunks and palm fronds.

The enemy fire again ceased.

The choppers circled the clearing. Doorgunners manned .50-caliber machine guns mounted in the slid-open side doors, the barrels of the weapons protruding like antennae sniffing the atmosphere.

"You figure there's anything left of these VC who have been firing on us, Lieutenant?" DeLuca asked.

No sounds, no movement came from either spot the two teams of the VC patrol had fired from.

"They could just be waiting to pick us off like sitting ducks, along with the chopper," said Hidalgo.

One of the Hueys banked out of its holding pattern to begin descending for a landing several hundred yards from the treeline, in the approximate middle of the clearing. The second gunship continued circling overhead, covering the first.

"We don't have much choice," said Gaines. "Let's find out."

He stormed from the treeline into the clearing, and the team went with him, spreading out from each other, charging into the windstorming backwash of the whirling chopper blades as the Huey touched down, resting lightly, quivering and throbbing like a big, metallic dragonfly.

When they were about one-third of the way to the chopper, Gaines again heard the telltale *ka-thump* of a firing mortar from behind them at the same instant that automatic fire started crackling from the jungle.

Then all was swallowed up by an explosion and a spurting column of fire as the mortar shell scored a direct hit on the waiting chopper.

A second explosion blew flaming chunks of razoring metal outward in every direction, but by that time Gaines and his team had thrown themselves down to hug the earth.

The instant the last pieces of debris had stopped falling, the team spun around to return fire at the VC patrol's positions.

"The sneaky bastards were playing possum after all," Hidalgo shouted above the yammering M-16 thundering in his fists and rocking his whole frame.

"Let's make 'em dead possums," DeLuca shouted back.

The remaining chopper looped around to sail by at tree-top level, the doorgunner blazing nonstop at the source of enemy fire.

The firing from the treeline tapered off as trees and vegetation were pulped under the heavy fire.

The chopper swooped around to bank in for a landing not far from where the first gunship sprouted smoke and flame from the ruin of its twisted, misshapen wreckage.

Gaines and his men ran like bats out of hell for the open side door of the chopper.

The AK-47s from the treeline opened up again.

"Damn," DeLuca snarled as they ran without slowing, "those boys don't give up easy."

"And neither do *we*," Gaines grunted.

They reached the chopper and flung themselves aboard,

the enemy fire drowned out in their ears as the doorgunner opened up with the .50-caliber.

"Let's go let's go let's go!" the doorgunner shouted at the pilot, his whole body shuddering under the powerful recoils of the pounding machine gun.

The pilot worked the controls as soon as he saw that the Tunnel Rats were aboard and sprawled across the deck. The gunship lifted sharply from the ground and the firing below.

Then the doorgunner's body caught a round from below. Gaines could tell from the way the gunner's body stumbled first this way, then that before it pitched out through the side door.

Gaines heard DeLuca and Hidalgo chorusing outraged, frustrated oaths. He flung himself past them and grasped the grips of the .50-caliber, swiveling it down and around, searching for targets.

He saw the sprawled body of the doorgunner where it lay crushed and broken from its fall. Then he saw the VC who had emerged from the treeline to fire with their AK-47s at the gunship pulling away overhead.

"Take us back for another pass!" Gaines shouted to the pilot over the throbbing racket of the chopper.

"You got it, pal," the pilot shouted back.

The Cong on the ground seemed almost surprised that the chopper banked around for a return engagement. Their firing after it had been more a show of defiance than anything else. They turned as one and started back for the cover of the jungle.

They never made it.

The gunship swooped past and Gaines hammered out one sustained burst, the big machine gun rocking his frame, spitting flame and fury and filling the air with ejected brass, eating up the ammo belt at a ferocious rate.

As the chopper whizzed by, Gaines caught a glimpse of the VC on the ground short of the treeline, as if they had stumbled. Both of their bodies had been practically blown apart by the fire from the .50-caliber.

Gaines eased off on the trigger. "Take us down," he called to the pilot.

"Aw hell, man, enough's enough," the pilot groused back. "You got those slopes, but that could still be a hot LZ down there."

"I think we've heard the last of them, at least from down there," Gaines replied. "We're going down for that doorgunner's body, then we're heading back to the base."

"You Gaines?" the pilot asked.

"I'm Gaines."

"Okay, Lieutenant, they told me this was your show. And he was a good doorgunner."

The pilot set them down near the doorgunner's body.

Gaines and DeLuca leaped from the chopper. They ran over to retrieve the broken corpse, DeLuca slipping his arms under the dead man's shoulders while Gaines grabbed hold of the ankles.

"This war doesn't need any more MIAs," DeLuca said.

They hustled back toward the chopper, carrying the body between them.

Hidalgo stood manning the mounted machine gun, Tu next to him, both of them watching the jungle keenly.

Gaines kept expecting to hear the crack of AK-47s opening up on them one more time, but it didn't happen. He and DeLuca reached the chopper, pulling the body aboard.

"All right, get us out of here," Gaines yelled to the pilot.

"Color us *gone*," the guy at the controls shouted back over his shoulder.

Then the chopper was lifting, the jungle treetops below them looking like an endless carpet of green.

Ngai Quang used the indentations on the sides of the access shaft for hand- and footholds.

The hole was at such an angle that the fiery red sun in the white sky stabbed directly into his eyes, blinding him.

For several seconds all he could hear was his own gasping for breath after the extreme physical exertion of his escape from the massive blast that had demolished the underground tunnel complex several thousand yards behind him. His heart pounded against his rib cage.

Then he heard the laughing sneer from the figure above. An American G.I. aimed a rifle at him.

"Well, if it ain't another gook. Come on up, slope, and join your buddies. Any funny shit and I'll blow your fucking head off."

Quang resumed climbing up out of the hole. He willed his heart to cease its pounding. He willed from his mind the images of his son's death.

Tsing had died before his eyes down there in the tunnels, within seconds of the alert that there was fighting above.

The blast had come as Quang and Tsing had crawled into a chamber where Quang's unit commanders had gathered to receive his instructions.

The layers of earth had dulled the intensity of the explosion, but the earth shook powerfully, and the men did not even have time to scream when the chamber collapsed and disappeared before Quang's eyes.

Quang had scuttled back to the exit tunnel whose existence was known only to himself, his son, and his commanders.

That frantic crawl to freedom, afraid that at any second

the tunnel he was in would cave in, filled his reeling mind and senses. He had witnessed again the death of his wife and other children, had seen himself pulling their crushed bodies from the rubble, the ones who had given his life meaning. And he saw his last image of Tsing swirling throughout these visions, dead, all of them dead, his command, everything gone. . . .

He reached the top of the access hole to the tunnel and pulled himself onto the surface.

They had intended to destroy the entire complex, thought Quang. The murderous filth. And they had demolished most of it. Tsing was dead. No! his mind commanded. Do not let your grief dull your reflexes!

The enemy had posted troops at the tunnel exits in case any escaped.

Lieutenant Pham had told the Americans everything about the tunnels. . . .

Quang had to squint in the glaring light of the sun. He saw the American, a hulking black fellow, motioning with his rifle.

"Raise 'em, slope. Raise 'em or you're dead meat."

Beyond the American, three other G.I.s stood, aiming their rifles at five of Captain Quang's people.

The five young Vietcong stood with their hands raised, covered from head to foot with the dirt and grime of the tunnels.

Quang raised his hands. He summoned up all of his self-control while he coiled up inside, ready to spring.

The American soldier motioned with his rifle for Quang to join the others. "Over there, charlie, and keep reaching for the sky. Any more of you buggers down there?"

Quang sidled over toward the others. He showed nothing but submission, but his every sense was focused on the G.I. waiting for the break.

The soldier kept his rifle aimed at Quang, but he momentarily shifted his eyes toward the mouth of the tunnel.

Quang pivoted on his straightened left leg almost faster than the eye could register, and far too fast for anyone to react. His right leg shot out as he emitted a curt snarl of pent-up rage. His right foot snapped the rifle from the soldier's hands.

The soldier registered startled surprise. He started to shout something to his men, but before he could, Quang left the ground with both feet and another shout, this time delivering a kick to the soldier's chest.

The American was knocked off his feet, the air gushing from his lungs. He landed, stunned, sprawled upon his back. He started to sit up.

The other Americans were turning to see what the commotion was, but by then Quang had already landed and, with the grace of a panther, he scooped up the M-16 dropped by the soldier.

Quang stepped over and planted one foot on the center of the American's chest, pushing him back down.

The black man was still stunned. He grunted in pain at the pressure of the foot, then looked up into the muzzle of his own M-16, which Quang aimed unwaveringly at the spot between the soldier's eyes, the muzzle less than six inches from the man's face.

"Oh, sweet Jesus," the soldier said. Beads of sweat popped out across his face.

His finger curled around the trigger, Quang called to the other Americans in heavily accented English. "You, drop your rifles!"

He only had to say it once.

Their eyes on the M-16 aimed at their sergeant, the other Americans dropped their rifles.

"Goddamnit, what are you doing?" the sergeant snarled

at his men from his prone position, defiantly ignoring the
rifle aimed at him. "Don't—"

It was too late.

Quang's men grabbed up the rifles, turning them on the
Americans.

"Kill them!" Quang shouted the command to his men in
their own tongue.

When the American soldiers realized that they were not
to be taken prisoner, they started a charge to wrest the
rifles from the Vietcong's hands.

The M-16s opened fire in a thunderous volley that
mowed down the Americans.

Quang turned from witnessing the slaughter and gazed
down the length of the rifle he aimed at the stoic mask that
was the face of the black soldier.

Quang thought of Tsing and the hundred others buried
alive in the tunnel complex behind him. He thought of his
wife, his youngest son, and his daughter. All of them dead,
and he left alive to suffer and to avenge them. His hatred
consumed him.

The American soldier beneath him saw what was coming. Quang saw his muscles start to bunch. In another second the soldier would have hurled himself away from the
rifle or done something to disarm Quang. But Quang didn't
give him the chance.

He squeezed the M-16's trigger. The assault rifle hammered and pounded in his grip. He fired an entire slip at
close range, utterly obliterating the soldier from midchest
upward in an unspeakable horror of splashing blood and
brains.

Quang leaned over. He stripped the body of ammunition, then turned to join his men as they did the same to the
three other dead Americans and also relieved the bodies of
their wallets.

The air hung heavy with the mingled stench of burnt cordite and bodies blown asunder.

"We must be gone from here," Quang said. His ears rang with the thunder of the rifle fire. "There are many Americans all around us."

One of the men turned his eyes back to the access hole to the tunnels.

"The others, Captain?"

"There is no hope for them," Quang said. "We are the only survivors. We must link up with another unit. But first we must avoid capture by the Americans. Into the jungle!" he ordered. "Quickly now, and without a sound!"

FOUR

Lieutenant Ngu Pham had lost track of time since having been taken into captivity by the Americans the evening before.

In the hours before dawn, he had been taken to a Quonset hut and been thrown bodily into a cell. His captors had locked him in and left him there as if forgotten.

He had fallen into a fitful sleep on the soiled cot and dreamed of his mother and father. He had heard nothing of them for several months. He hoped they were alive, and his sister and her husband. He missed them very much, and for so long now he had been unable to think of anything else but home, especially when he was in the tunnels.

He had awoken to the clanging of his cell door's being opened. He felt the aches and pains from the rough handling he had received at the hands of the American field patrol he had stumbled onto.

They had seen him and captured him before he'd had a chance to flee. They had punched him, shoved him, and kicked him during the course of bringing him in to the base at Lai Khe.

Pham somehow understood. He knew how they felt. He, too, had seen the bodies of his friends, had seen and heard the wounded screaming their agony because there was no painkiller, no medicine. He was weary of the killing, weary of war, to the marrow of his bones, to his soul.

The tunnels, too, had worked to eat away at his nerves until he had no appetite and could not sleep. But he had not worked up the courage to confront his fears, could not bring himself to ask Captain Quang to relieve him of duty.

Lieutenant Pham was twenty years old. He cared very much what others thought of him. He could not imagine having to endure disgrace in the eyes of his comrades and family members when he returned home.

The night before, Pham and his patrol had been working their way behind the American lines, and had slipped from the tunnels when darkness cloaked the jungle.

In the hot, humid darkness, Pham had led them into the sights of a Special Forces sniper team. The unit had died under a withering hail of well-paced rounds.

Pham had dived away for cover, had felt a round tug at a pants leg and the warm sizzle of another bullet that traced a hairline nick across the top of his right ear. But he had gotten away and he had decided then and there to run and not stop until he was safe on some mountain where he could catch his breath and gather his wits.

It was then that he had run into the patrol that captured him and brought him here.

He was frightened. He was terrified. He thought they would kill him.

They had not needed force to make him talk. He had been too close to the edge already. They had only to show him the machine with the electrodes and assure him that he would never be the same, would never want to know a woman after what the machine would do to him.

And so he had talked.

He had told them, through a Viet interpreter, what he knew about the tunnel complex that was Captain Quang's underground base, including the location of the escape tunnels, feeling ashamed to the point of tears at his betrayal of his comrades.

The Americans would send in the Tunnel Rats.

That alone, Pham knew, would most likely seal the fate of Captain Quang and his command. He would be responsible for the deaths of all those caught in the tunnels.

All Pham had wanted was to escape, to return home.

Service as a guerrilla fighter for the Vietcong had been exciting at first for a boy fresh from the farm. He did not much care about politics. His family had been peasants for generations. There had been the pleasure of fellowship, the excitement of setting ambushes for Americans, who seemed to Pham wholly unequipped to deal with jungle combat.

And there had been other things. Many young women worked and fought in the service of the Vietcong. There was more opportunity for Pham to find girls who would sleep with him.

But when it soured for him, when the fighting tapered off because of the Americans' superior firepower, and there were no girls and only long days sweltering, cramped, stifled in the tunnels . . . He wanted out, yes, but he had made friends among those he served with in the tunnels, and he wished them no ill will.

And yet, when the Americans had threatened him with pain, he had nearly passed out, had nearly wet himself as he listened to their words.

He had had enough of war. He could take no more. He

was a broken man. He had not escaped. He could never escape from what he had done, he told himself. He would never see his parents, his home, again. He was doomed.

The same pair of soldiers who had locked him up now led him from his cell in the Quonset and across the busy base beneath the oppressive sun. They took him to the same fortified bunker where he had been questioned the night before.

Outside the bunker stood two ARVN soldiers.

Inside, Pham did not recognize any of the men as being among those who had interrogated him last night.

There were four Americans present: a captain in pressed fatigues, and three men who looked and smelled as if they had just come in from the field. There was the faint smell of death about them.

Tunnel Rats, thought Pham.

With the Americans was an ARVN officer in a freshly pressed uniform.

"Ah, Lieutenant Pham, is it?" The ARVN officer addressed Pham in their native tongue. "You have done a good thing, young man, in coming to the aid of your country and its allies."

Pham tried to find his voice but could not at first. He cleared his throat. "Captain Quang?" he asked.

"Assumed dead, with most of his men. Thanks to you, Lieutenant. You did the right thing. The entire underground command structure was destroyed thanks to the work of these men here." The Viet officer nodded to the grimy, disheveled American soldiers Pham had guessed to be Tunnel Rats.

Pham felt a sinking feeling in his stomach. "What is to happen to me?" he asked, already knowing the answer.

"You are in my custody. I am Major Van Dow. You will be held for further interrogation."

Pham tried to ward off a feeling of resignation. "But they will kill me! The Vietcong—"

"Is there some problem?" the American captain asked Dow.

Pham knew some English, enough to sense the gist of what was being said.

"He is afraid of reprisal from the Cong," said Major Van Dow. "Do not worry, Captain Carter. Our intelligence section will make better progress interrogating him further because of the language barrier, and he will be guarded around the clock. I will assign Lieutenant Xong to see to his protection. Xong is my best man."

Pham noticed that Carter was over six feet tall, broad through the shoulders, though not heavy. He addressed the captain directly in faltering English.

"I do as you ask. I tell you all about tunnels. Let me go. I only want to go home."

"That's all any of us want," Carter told him, "but you're a prisoner of war, sport, and it's out of my hands. Your VC ass belongs to Major Dow. That's regulations."

Van Dow snapped a command at his men.

The two ARVN soldiers stepped in from outside, and each grabbed Pham by one arm.

Pham's eyes dropped to the ground, and he felt despair. *I am doomed,* he said to himself.

The ARVN regulars led him from the bunker.

Lieutenant Gaines watched Pham being led away without too much interest. He was too worn out to care.

His primary concern at the moment was getting out of his funky fatigues and under a hot shower.

There were too many good G.I.s shipped home in body bags for him to feel any sympathy for a VC, informer or otherwise, and he knew Carter, Hidalgo, and DeLuca felt the same way.

"Well, I guess that's that," said Carter. He looked at the Tunnel Rats team. "You did a good job, men."

"Just don't let the desk men raise a stink about there being no body count," said Hidalgo.

"Yeah." DeLuca nodded. "Buried alive is just what those VC fuckers had coming to 'em. If the pencil pushers want a body count, they can trade in their pencils for shovels and go to work."

"They'll be happy enough to know that Quang and his battalion have been put out of commission," said Carter.

"I just hope to hell Quang was buried in that cave-in," said Gaines. "Not knowing is the one thing bad about taking out a complex the way we greased that one."

Major Van Dow nodded. "It would be most unfortunate if Captain Quang managed to somehow escape. He is a brilliant strategist and an inspiring leader. He would truly inspire respect if he were to survive. He would pose a serious problem."

"We've got enough of those already," said Carter, "and it's about time we scored big. You men haven't failed me yet," he told the Tunnel Rats. "You score with every mission I give you. But you may have noticed that I've been giving you less and less."

"That ain't so bad," Hidalgo said. "Gives me a chance to catch up on my reading."

"Yeah," DeLuca snorted. "*Batman* and *Archie*."

"If that were the extent of it," said Gaines, "I wouldn't mind either, but what it could mean is that charlie's got someone who's tipping him off anytime we get close to finding out about another set of tunnels."

"In other words, a spy," said Carter.

"Could this be connected with our other problem of missing supplies and armament?" asked Major Van Dow.

There had been increasing instances of theft from the base in recent weeks.

"The possibility of a spy in our midst always exists," said Carter. "Perhaps Lieutenant Pham may be able to shed some light on that subject."

"I will see to it immediately," said Van Dow. He about-faced and left the bunker.

"And why don't we see about hitting the showers," said Gaines.

"I was about to suggest that very thing," said Carter, wrinkling his nose. "You may proceed, Lieutenant. And again, congratulations to you and your men on a job extremely well done."

Quang and the small group with him pressed themselves against the ground that sloped away from the road.

The elephant grass, growing right up to the edge of the road, helped to conceal them from sight.

A U.S. Army armored personnel carrier rumbled past.

The area had been thick with American activity in the immediate wake of the underground explosion that had destroyed the tunnel complex and most of Quang's command.

He and the men with him had made their way through it all, putting a distance of more than one and a half kilometers between themselves and the spot where they had killed the American patrol during their escape.

The shooting of the American soldier had had a cathartic effect on Quang. His grief at the loss of Tsing and all of his other suffering were submerged beneath the cool command he took of the situation.

They had hidden as helicopters had buzzed the treetops overhead. They had stealthily slipped away from the American and ARVN forces swarming across the area.

They had almost reached their destination and were

about to cross the road when they heard the approach of the vehicle and dived for cover.

Quang motioned the five other men to remain where they were for another thirty seconds after the vehicle passed. Then he was on his feet, and his men followed him across the road where the land dropped off sharply.

They worked their way down to where a peasant hut stood amid a cluster of balsa trees, well removed from sight by the trees and the terrain.

A farmer and his wife stood waiting for Quang and his group in front of the hut.

"You expected us?" asked Quang.

"Word reached us of the destruction of your tunnel complex," the farmer said. "We did not think you would be so easy to destroy, Captain Quang. You had told us to expect you in the event of an emergency. We are here."

Quang marveled again at the communications network the civilian populace provided, and of the widespread support in the rural hamlets for the Vietcong.

"You are prepared for us, then?"

"This way," said the farmer.

He led them into the humble hut. He pushed aside a crude wood table, flung aside a faded square rug, and opened a trapdoor in the bare wood floor.

The light of day shone down on a space dug out from the ground. The walls and floor were of dirt, but a blanket had been laid down as a carpet. This was one of several hideaways Quang had arranged for himself in the region surrounding the tunnel complex.

Quang motioned his men into the chamber, then said to the farmer and his wife, "You have done well. My men and I will impose upon your hospitality only until darkness falls."

"It is hardly an imposition, Captain Quang," said the wife. "We are proud to offer our help."

"Your son Tsing," said the farmer, "is he coming behind you?"

"You knew my son?"

The farmer's expression grew grave at Quang's use of the past tense. "I am among those who supply rice to those who work for Tsing, digging the tunnel beneath the base at Lai Khe. Your son is a good man."

"My son is dead. He was buried alive when the Americans blew up the tunnels."

"Our deepest sympathies, Captain Quang," said the farmer's wife.

"How else may we be of assistance?" asked her husband. "We will do anything we can to help."

"I must get word to the other commanders immediately that I am alive," said Quang.

"We can see to that."

"Work on the tunnel beneath the base must continue. My son told me before he died that the work was near completion. I shall personally take command of that."

"I will take word to the digging teams personally," the wife said. "You can depend on us, Captain Quang."

"I know I can," Quang told them. "It is why the American imperialists will never be victorious over us no matter their numbers and their machines of war. It is because of you that they will be driven from our land."

"Do not speak, please, my captain, of what we have done. You have given your son to the cause only this day, and you speak of carrying on the fight to victory."

"I will grieve when the fight is won," said Quang. "Now I think only of vengeance; for my family, for my son, and for all of those who died this morning in the tunnels the Americans destroyed. I am certain their information came from an informant and that his name is Lieutenant Pham. Pham must be found and silenced."

"I shall see to it," the farmer promised him.

"And there is one final thing," said Quang, "and to me it is the most important. My tunnels, my men, my son . . . they were destroyed by Tunnel Rats. It could have been no other. I want to know who was personally responsible for blowing up those tunnels. Contact our man on the base at Lai Khe. It should be easy enough to learn the name of the team leader. It is a personal thing now between that man and me. A blood duel to the finish, and he does not even know it yet. When I learn the name of the man responsible, I will not rest until he is dead."

FIVE

Lai Khe was located twenty-five miles due north of Saigon along Highway 13, which cut through the steep, rugged, forested foothills of the central highlands that stretched up to North Vietnam.

Lai Khe was home to the U.S. 1st Infantry Division and the ARVN 5th Division, placed down smack dab in the middle of terrain that was considered secured during the daylight hours but that belonged to whoever possessed the most skill, stealth, and luck after the sun went down.

The base occupied a square quarter mile, the perimeter strung with concertina wire decorated with empty beer cans. The idea was that sentries would be alerted to any attempted nighttime penetration by the sounds of the cans against the wire.

Sandbagged defensive positions, placed at regular intervals along the perimeter, held a variety of heavy firepower: M-79 machine guns, mortars, rockets, all trained on a five-hundred-foot killing area that separated the perimeter from the jungle.

Ann Bradley stood in front of the plywood-frame emergency room of the ambulatory hospital unit at Lai Khe. She wore fatigues and a flack jacket.

She saw Scott Gaines leaving Captain Carter's bunker with DeLuca and Hidalgo.

Gaines looked her way, saw her, and said something to the men of his team.

They spoke to him for a moment, obviously ribbing him about something, and she guessed that it had to do with her. Then both of them sent her a friendly wave and continued off away from Gaines in the direction of the hooch shared by the three men of the Tunnel Rats team.

Gaines worked his way toward her through the maze of activity on the base, activity that had worn away the grass everywhere within the perimeter and bared rocky red soil, the dust of which coated everything.

Things had slowed down to a stop in the E.R., and so she had stepped outside for some fresh air, for a break, and to watch—she could not deny it—for Gaines after she had heard that Scott's team was back from its mission.

You took your breaks when you could. With little or no notice you could find yourself working a twelve- or fifteen-hour shift once the Medevac choppers started ferrying in the wounded.

Then the E.R. became pure bedlam, a scene of doctors and nurses running from stretcher to stretcher to make rushed, superficial examinations, deciding in what order to begin operating.

Those with lesser wounds were patched up and sent to Saigon to mend. The ones who were worse off were choppered at once to a more definitive care unit.

It was difficult for Ann Bradley to remember the naive,

country-bred kid who had gone to the hayseed nursing school fourteen months ago. That seemed so long ago, so far away.

The Army recruiter had come to the nursing school. She had attended the talk. Nurses were needed. They would not be in the combat zone, but they were needed desperately to serve their country.

It was her first time away from home for any extended period of time. She came from a good family. She thought well of her mother and father and wished there were some way she could convey to them through her letters what it was like being in-country, but it was beyond her powers to describe to them what she was going through, what her life was like. And even if she could have described it, she knew it would have been beyond their comprehension. She knew this because it would have been beyond the comprehension of the kid she had been only fourteen months ago.

You did what you could, but it was not enough. It was never enough.

Ann Bradley had never heard of Vietnam until her brother had been sent there in the marines. She had been harboring a vague uneasiness that she was not shouldering her share of a struggle against her nation's enemies.

The kid fresh off the farm had signed up on the spot.

She had been in-country for seven months, and had grown up in a hurry.

The recruiters had lied, of course, about nurses' not being deployed to a combat zone. And there was at least one rocket attack per week on Lai Khe. There were firefights nearly every night in the jungle surrounding the base.

With the passing stream of screaming, dying young men, with the threat constantly there that the next rocket charlie fired into the base could have your name on it, the pressure inside built and built. Ann had seen people who she thought better than herself at handling stress, ultimately break.

There were only so many ways you could deal with the pressure, counter the despair, if you were stationed at Lai Khe.

There was booze. There was pot and hard drugs. There was partying with a desperate abandon that she found only depressing.

She was not exactly sure she knew what was holding her together, what with the day-to-day hell that was her life. Gaines had something to do with it, she knew that much, even though they had not yet slept together.

As she watched Gaines nearing her, something about the way he moved reminded her of a jungle beast, all sinew and muscle, grace and savagery combined.

She thought, *Maybe tonight*, and had to bite her lower lip to hold back a chuckle at her lasciviousness.

Life in a war zone had changed her awareness and perception of a lot of things. Mother would not approve, she thought wryly.

She had slept with only one man during her time in-country—Philip Stevens, one of the doctors of the unit, a nice, fine man who was in the process of being destroyed by the war and destroying himself with alcohol.

It had not taken her long to realize that she was sleeping with that man not out of her feeling for him but rather as a way of coping with her fears. She had not thought that fair to either of them, and they had broken off intimate relations, amicably, two months ago.

She was still very fond of the man, but she had learned to cope with fear by ignoring it and submerging herself wholly in her work, giving herself no time to fret and despair.

That was where she'd been when she'd met Gaines through a mutual acquaintance about a month ago.

They had taken to each other right off. He was a nice guy. Her kind of guy. You could talk ideas with him, not just about the weather and the price of eggs. He was a thoroughly competent individual—with an emphasis on the *individual* part, she thought wryly—who was tough enough to wade through fields without succumbing to enemy fire or to the dehumanization that could erode the strongest and best of men.

They were kindred spirits. Their opinions differed on enough things to offer lively conversations, which they both enjoyed. They had a mutual respect for each other's intellect. They agreed on most of the important things and enjoyed each other's company. They had become very good friends. He had helped her to realize that by avoiding all human contact and doing nothing but burying herself in her work, she was in fact putting herself on the same road to burnout and self-destruction as Stevens.

The only things that had kept her from becoming a bit bolder with Gaines were his old-fashioned chivalrous attitude and her concerns about becoming emotionally involved with a man who could be brought back to the base in a body bag any day, or be brought in to die before her eyes on one of the operating tables of the E.R.

But you're already committed to him, already emotionally involved with him, she told herself.

Maybe tonight, she thought again with a small grin to herself as he reached her.

There was a breeze picking up, so she could not really smell the death and violence on him. But she knew it was there, could see it in his eyes when he got up close, and she wondered if she should have beckoned him.

Her concerns vanished when he registered a lopsided smile of greeting, bone-weary but thoroughly real.

"Ah, a civilized person at last. Hi, Ann. How's the war treating you?" The bedraggled condition of his fatigues and the grime smeared across his face and hands had become apparent only once he'd gotten closer.

"Better than it's been treating you, I'd say. Are you okay, Scott?"

The lopsided grin stayed in place. "Nothing a date with my favorite nurse wouldn't cure."

"It'll have to be tonight. I'm on all day, and tomorrow Phil and I are due to spend the afternoon at Hoa Phu."

Gaines had been unable to dissuade her from extending her work hours to include one day per week spent in neighboring villages where she and Stevens dispensed rudimentary medical treatment to civilians.

This was done with the approval of their superiors, who provided supplies and transportation, viewing the goodwill endeavor as another small attempt at gaining the hearts and minds of the civilian populace.

"How's Phil doing?" Gaines asked.

"He's doing fine, Scott." She wasn't sure what to say. "He's doing fine. . . . He's . . . about the way you saw him last time."

"That isn't good." Gaines frowned. "Maybe the three of us should go out on the town one of these nights, go into Saigon, get him away from all of this for a little bit. We could talk to him."

It was a mark of the man, thought Ann Bradley, that he should be as weary as he appeared to be, as battered in body and psyche as only combat could render a man, and yet be able to express genuine concern for another human being in a very personal, private kind of trouble.

She could not help herself. She touched the side of his

face with the palm of her hand, a gesture of open affection she had never shown him before.

"You're quite a guy, do you know that, Lieutenant? But tonight I need my escape, and I'd like to make that escape with you. Sure, Scott, a night on the town with you sounds great to me."

Twice a day the Division ran a bus into Saigon along Highway 13, which was more or less secure at all times. The evening bus left the base with an armed escort at precisely 1800 hours and left Saigon for the half-hour return trip home at 2300 hours, the idea being that curtailing some of the more raucous partyers before midnight made for fewer hangovers in the ranks the following morning.

"You're on," said Gaines. "Meet you at the bus at eighteen hundred?"

"It's a date," she said.

She started to say some more, started to tell him to take care of himself, for he did look like a man just in from the killing fields who needed to refresh body and spirit.

She was interrupted by an intensifying of the sound around the base as two helicopters rotored in for landings several hundred yards from the E.R.

Corpsmen were already sprinting, wheeling gurneys toward the choppers, where soldiers were handing down bodies that could be wounded or dead, freshly evacuated from somewhere a few miles away where fighting raged.

"Tonight," said Gaines, "if you can get away."

She nodded acknowledgment and hurried back into the emergency room.

Ky knew he might anger Khong Noh by disturbing him, and angering the brutish boss of this band of bandits was something Ky did not want to do. But he reasoned he might just as easily court Khong Noh's displeasure by not giving him the information he had just received.

He stood outside Khong Noh's tent and cleared his throat.

"Uh, my leader, there is something you should know."

"Eh, what's that?" came Khong Noh's weary-sounding voice.

There was sluggish movement, the rustle of material, and a moment later Khong Noh appeared, holding back one flap of the tent, clad only in his trousers.

Ky glimpsed a young woman, a teenaged girl actually, sprawled facedown at an unusual angle half on and half off Khong Noh's sleeping bag. She was unconscious, or perhaps worse off, thought Ky. Her body was covered with bruises, her legs widely, crudely spread apart.

She had been one of the girls taken alive from the last raid they had gone on, two nights before. Ky had killed the women he had raped as the village had burned.

Khong Noh was big for a Vietnamese. He ruled through brute strength and cunning. He had a sagging belly, his face was scarred and pockmarked, and his expression glowered with brooding brutality. Exactly the type of man it took to rule this band of eight cutthroats who had lived off the land, looting and pillaging without capture for more than three years, thought Ky.

Some of the men were ARVN deserters; some were underworld characters from Saigon who had crossed one associate too many and could not go back. Others, like Ky, had simply been uprooted, displaced by the war, their structured lives yanked out from under them, sometimes cruelly.

Ky had been a farmer. His home, like those of his neighbors, had been burned to the ground by something called napalm, which was dropped from the jet planes that had soared by low overhead one day three years earlier while Ky had been working in the communal garden. His wife and four children had been in their home. Only their charred, skeletal remains had been left after the fires burned out.

Ky had never been the same.

He had joined Khong Noh's gang soon after. At first he had killed to vent his anger, and in the killing of others, he had realized at once, he was killing the things within him that were humane, compassionate.

At first he had wondered how the men of the gang could be so brutal, could commit such horrible atrocities as they did during raids. But killing came easy after the first few, even after the rage had been vented, the sorrow and grief of his loss relegated to a constant ache. Before long he was truly one of them, slaughtering for what he stole, often killing for pleasure, expecting at any time that he would be the next to die.

"I have just received word of an American convoy due to pass through Hoa Phu tomorrow morning," Ky informed Khong Noh. "We were only today discussing that we will soon be running low on ammunition, and there is always a need for more weapons. You also mentioned that Hoa Phu is ripe for picking."

"This word on the convoy," said Khong Noh. "Can your information be trusted?"

"The information comes directly from Lieutenant Xong himself," said Ky.

Xong was an ARVN officer stationed at nearby Lai Khe. Ky and Khong Noh were well aware that Xong also supplied information to the Vietcong. Xong had in fact made no secret of this when he had approached Noh eighteen months earlier with his proposition to sell useful information.

Ky sensed a stirring behind Noh, deeper in the tent. He looked in over Noh's shoulder.

The girl sprawled across the sleeping bag had regained consciousness. She rolled over onto her back. Her face was bruised, puffy from repeated beatings during repeated rapes. Her eyes darted around the interior of the tent.

The girl spied Noh's bayonet, which lay near the sleeping bag, next to his rifle and a holstered pistol. She grabbed the bayonet and with a blindly enraged shriek flung herself at Noh, raising the bayonet, holding it by the handle to swing it at him.

Noh turned in time. He reached out with his left hand and grasped the girl's hand. He placed a foot behind one of her legs and pushed her hand with the palm of his right hand. She tripped over his foot and fell to the ground, and he fell down atop her.

As Ky watched, Khong Noh ripped the bayonet from the girl's hand. He commenced plunging it into her chest angrily, raising the bayonet high over his head and slashing down at her over and over and over again, the blade making wet, meaty sounds. His ragged, gasping breathing sounded to Ky like that of a man engaged in rough intercourse.

The girl screamed once, struggled briefly, gurgled, and lay still.

Noh stabbed her several times after she was dead, and left the bayonet sticking out of the center of her bloody, destroyed left breast. He stood. He spat down on her corpse and turned to Ky, the front of his trousers smeared with the girl's blood.

"Remove her."

Ky eased into the tent. He removed the bayonet, lifted the limp body of the girl, and threw it over his shoulder. He stepped back out of the tent.

"Treacherous whore," Noh said with a last look at the corpse. "And I had not yet satiated myself. Is there not a woman left from the last raid?"

"Yes, my leader. You said the men could share her among them."

"Have her sent to me. And tell the men to prepare for an attack tomorrow on Hoa Phu and on the American convoy."

SIX

The tunnel that Tsing's digging crew had been working on for the past several weeks began in a dip in the terrain a considerable distance beyond the perimeter of the base at Lai Khe and the killground surrounding it.

Quang met the crew shortly after darkness claimed the land.

The crew numbered half a dozen: university-age men and women from the surrounding villages. They were dressed in black and carried shoulder-strapped AK-47s.

They cleared back foliage, revealing for Quang the tunnel entrance, which angled into the earth diagonally in the direction of the military installation nearby. Then they went down into the close quarters and stale air of the tunnel and, with a bare minimum of conversation, resumed work by the illumination of flashlights.

The digging crew worked diligently with barely a rest. They tacitly accepted Quang as their commander.

Quang itched inside with anticipation. An examination

of the crew's progress before tonight's work began had made him realize how close his son's team had been to achieving their goal.

The diggers were directly beneath the base!

They dug and filled woven baskets, which were promptly carried away and replaced by empty ones. Other diggers rushed to build reinforcements with pieces of lumber. The tunnel had to be wide enough for the attackers to carry rifles. They worked quickly.

Sweating, straining, struggling, the diggers moved upward. They worked more slowly now, taking great care to make as little noise as possible, a necessity if they hoped to gain the surface without discovery by anyone on the grounds inside the base.

Quang was taking a break just outside the mouth of the tunnel, standing by himself, when he distinguished a particular bird warble that stood apart slightly from the ongoing chatter of jungle nightlife around him.

He tensed. He reached for his rifle, which leaned against the trunk of a balsa tree next to him.

He had placed four sentries around the mouth of the tunnel. The sentries' hidden positions in the heavy forestation formed a rectangle, with the tunnel, and Quang, in the approximate center.

The nightbird sound was in fact the warning signal of one of the sentries.

Quang listened closely, and when the warble came again, he placed it as coming from the sentry placed to his left, to the northeast, the direction away from the lights of Lai Khe.

He heard the faint shifting of branches and could barely make out the sounds of someone approaching.

The sounds, the movement, ceased.

A voice whispered, "I am Lieutenant Xong. Is Captain Quang here?"

Quang held the flashlight well away from his body. He flicked it on and off once, very quickly, to make his position for the man he could not see. He recognized the voice.

"It is I, Lieutenant."

Xong stepped forward, coming to stand next to Quang, where Quang could distinguish a narrow face atop a body in civilian clothes that was somehow effeminate despite being muscular. Quang had never liked the man.

"Captain Quang, I was most sorry to hear about the fate of your son and the men of your command," Xong said with a slight lisp.

"What news?" Quang demanded curtly.

Xong must have stolen away from the ARVN division based at Lai Khe and circled around to make sure he was not being followed to his meeting with a Vietcong commander.

"A Lieutenant Pham was captured," said Xong. "It was he who told the Americans about the tunnels."

Xong commanded a cell of Vietcong sympathizers within the ARVN ranks at Lai Khe. Some of these were soldiers who worked with the American troops, who had regular, easy access to the American facilities. These were the men who had managed to steal ammunition and supplies from right under the Americans' noses. It was one such man who had supplied Xong with the information he was now passing on to Captain Quang.

"The only thing we have to be thankful for is that Pham does not know about this tunnel," said Quang. "What is the current status of Lieutenant Pham?"

Quang thought he detected in the faint light a smirk that crinkled Xong's thin, cruel lips.

"He is being detained in a cell at Division headquarters

until tomorrow morning, when he is scheduled to be trans-
ferred to Saigon."

"He must be made to pay for his betrayal before they
remove him from Lai Khe."

"I shall see to it," Xong assured him. "Lieutenant Pham
will not leave Lai Khe alive."

"The digging here will be completed tonight," said
Quang. "We shall adhere to Tsing's original schedule. We
will attack the base tomorrow night through the tunnel."

"I shall be prepared to assist in whatever way I can,
Captain."

"It is important that you do not openly show your
hand," Quang warned. "Not only would you greatly endanger yourself, but you have become a most vital source of
information, Lieutenant, not to mention your assistance in
helping us to acquire goods and ammunition from the
American supplies."

"That is something else that must be discussed," said
Xong. "The Americans have taken action to stop the
losses. They suspect a spy in the ARVN ranks. Major Van
Dow has assigned me to investigate the matter."

Again the hint of a smirk.

"That will put you in an ideal position to stall such an
investigation," said Quang. "Perhaps you will find someone else more deserving than yourself to take the blame."

"I was thinking the same thing, Captain. As you say, an
ideal position."

Quang's features grew grave. "There is one piece of
information I need to know. You know what it is."

Xong nodded. "The name of the man who led the destruction of your tunnels. The man responsible for the
death of your son."

"You know his name?"

"I do."

"Do not banter with me, Lieutenant." Quang's lowered voice hardened to cold steel. "You are a loyal ally of the People's Army of the Socialist Republic, but nothing, nothing, will stand in my way of avenging Tsing's death."

"I do not banter, Captain. I only wish you to remember my assistance when this war is over. The Americans will be driven out. The government will be toppled. We shall be victorious and you shall hold much power. It is then that I shall accept any payment or reward you may choose to bestow for the assistance I am about to lend you in avenging your son's death."

"Tell me what you know." Quang's voice remained chilly.

"The man you want is a Lieutenant Scott Gaines," said Xong. "He is attached to the Americans' 1st Infantry Division at Lai Khe."

"The Tunnel Rats." Quang spat the phrase as if it were a profanity.

Xong nodded. "I can offer you more assistance than merely a name," he said.

"Then offer it."

"I know where Lieutenant Gaines will be tonight."

"Tell me," Quang demanded.

Xong had dealt personally with Quang on numerous occasions. This was the first time he had ever discerned anything remotely resembling emotion.

"One of my men overheard Lieutenant Gaines using a base telephone," said Xong. "The lieutenant was calling a restaurant in Saigon, making reservations for this evening."

"Then there is no time to lose," Quang snapped. "You should have given me this information first. The details now, quickly. I must make arrangements."

"What do you intend to do, Captain?"

"I said the details *quickly*, Lieutenant. I will dispatch our best gunmen into Saigon. Lieutenant Gaines and whoever is with him will not leave that restaurant alive."

Gaines and Ann Bradley rode the evening bus into Saigon that evening as planned.

Gaines, in freshly pressed khaki, felt completely refreshed from the rigors of combat much earlier that day.

Ann wore civvies, a denim skirt, and a red blouse that managed to look casual and elegant at the same time and displayed a fine figure to fine advantage.

They began the evening with a leisurely stroll through the exotic flower market in Nguyen-Hue Street, renowned throughout the country for the elegant displays in long rows of booths.

The capital of South Vietnam, a neon cluster sprawling in all directions from the head of a forty-mile inlet connecting the harbor with the Pacific Ocean, had swollen to a wartime population of five million.

Gaines offered to buy Ann every flower in the place, but Ann settled for a single long-stemmed rose.

They flagged down a trishaw. Gaines gave the address of the restaurant to the coolie and they were off, heading along busy Duong Tu-Do—Liberty Street, the main street of Saigon—a broad boulevard leading directly from the docks to a cathedral, bisecting the downtown area.

Modern business buildings dwarfed huts standing between the newer structures. The streets were alive with cars, trucks, trishaws, pedicabs, and countless bicycles. Itinerant vendors wandered in hordes, shrilly hawking their wares. Groups of men squatted on the sidewalks, playing games of chance.

Vietnamese women were said to be the most beautiful of the Orient. Here, the respectable ones wore brightly colored sheathlike dresses. The prostitutes were everywhere, dressed in the exaggerated sexuality of the oldest profession, calling out to every American male in sight with the exception of Gaines, who obviously had no need of female companionship.

This was the third time Gaines and Ann had gone to Chez Louis, an elegant holdover from the days of French colonialism. The place was no less pricey than any of the other restaurants thriving on the boom economy of Saigon, but the food was good, damn good—even if Gaines didn't know a whole hell of a lot about French cuisine—and that in itself made it stand out in a town where exclusivity and quality did not always go hand in hand.

The place was sandwiched in at ground level, midblock, flanked to one side by an Indian grocer's and on the other by a Chinese bazaar that offered a range of goods, everything from clothing to jewelry to dried fish.

They had an excellent dinner of filet mignon, each of them savoring their dinner and the warmth of companionship. The conversation skipped effortlessly, pleasurably, from books read to recollections of back home to the sights and experiences shared thus far this day and evening.

They talked about everything except their work, the war, the way they spent their days.

This was an escape, a pause, however brief, in the hellish existence of Lai Khe and a dirty little jungle war. At that moment, all that somehow seemed a million miles away to Scott Gaines.

They had polished off a dessert of napoleons and were dawdling over after-dinner snifters of liqueur when she got around to the subject she had come here to discuss.

Gaines was not a drinking man. Maybe a 3.2 beer on a day off, but that was about it. He enjoyed the relaxed glow he felt from the dinner and liqueur, but he was not so relaxed that he lowered his awareness of the scene around their booth, as alert for any signs of danger from the murmuring conversations and activity as he would be had they been in the middle of the jungle.

Gaines understood that this war did not end at the jungle. He understood that there was a human jungle in this city every bit as dangerous as the primitive terrain surrounding it.

Even so, he was aware of what Ann was talking about, because he had been thinking about it, too. But it seemed like centuries since he'd felt this way about a woman, since well before he'd enlisted and been sent to the Nam.

"Do you realize, Lieutenant Gaines, that we have spent this evening discussing everything under the sun, but we haven't once talked about us?"

Gaines glanced at his watch. "Uh, we'd better be flagging ourselves out of here if we want to catch that bus back to the base."

She grinned, sighed exaggeratedly. "I knew you'd be flippant when I brought it up." She reached across the table and rested warm, slender fingers across his rough, bruised hand. "When I brought *us* up."

He grinned back at her. He did like this gal, he told himself again. Maybe . . . more than liked, he told himself.

"So you've got me figured out. What's happening here, kid? Are we pushing this thing a little further to see what happens next?"

"I don't know. Are we?"

"You started this," he reminded her.

She said, "Everyone who knows us thinks we're sleeping together."

"Not the ones who really know us," he corrected. "They know we're just friends. But I know what you mean, Ann. I've been thinking about us too."

"Now, that is interesting. I'd been wondering if you were."

"How could I not? I feel this thing we've got between us too. I haven't felt this comfortable with a whole lot of people. I guess I'm not real sure what to make of it, considering the circumstances. Lai Khe isn't exactly a street block back in the World."

Their eyes connected, held.

"We could be more than friends," she said, not removing her hand from his.

"There's everything else, this rotten damn war," he said. "I don't know, Ann. I'm not sure it would do either of us any good to really fall in love and then lose the other one when it came our time to catch a bullet."

"A time and a place for everything." She nodded, not breaking eye contact.

"Maybe that's it."

"Or maybe we need each other, Scott, the way a man and a woman need each other to make themselves feel something besides fear and pain. An affirmation of life. That's something that's awful hard to come by in-country these days."

"I've thought about us that way," said Gaines. "It's not that I don't want you."

"Well, I'm certainly glad to hear that," she teased.

"You'll find out how much you turn me on, lady, the first time I let myself go. Believe it."

Her eyes sparkled. So did her smile. "Oh, I believe it. And it is nice to hear you admit there will be a first time."

Gaines felt himself turning warm in the face. He hoped to almighty hell that he was not blushing. He'd had his share of good-time frolics with the opposite sex. He'd had no trouble finding girls to run with in high school and college and after.

But yeah, it had been one hell of a long time, and it occurred to him for the first time that he could well be losing touch more than he realized with the way civilized people behaved in peacetime, everyday situations. He hadn't thought much on that before, and the thought popped through his mind now that, if he managed to survive this war, going back to the existence of a noncombatant might take some adjusting to.

"I haven't admitted anything," he chided, "though I will admit the idea is fraught with potential."

"'Fraught with potential.'" She grinned, shook her head at him. "You may be thinking too much, guy. In affairs of the heart, logic is not always applicable."

He glanced at his watch again but took care not to remove his hand from hers.

"In this case, it might be," he said. "We miss that bus back to the base and we're AWOL."

"All right, Mr. Time and Place," she conceded, "but here's another saying. Call it food for thought. 'Gather your rosebuds while ye may.' I haven't been this comfortable with a whole lot of people either, Scott, in this madhouse war or back home. I'd just hate to think that our lives brushed together and that we saw what was there and that we let it go at that. See, no logic."

"Women's logic," he corrected. "And yeah, plenty of food for thought, but I wasn't kidding about missing that bus, Nurse Bradley. We'd better get a move on."

SEVEN

Vo Tran left Chinh and Tho with the dilapidated Citröen parked across the street and a half block away from the Chez Louis.

He wended his way through the pedestrian and vehicular traffic flooding the street even at this late hour.

While the city's red-light district throbbed with activity twenty-four hours a day, this was a more respectable district, and the restaurants and shops would begin closing soon as American G.I.s began drifting back toward their bases.

Tran gained the opposite sidewalk. He did not approach the restaurant along the sidewalk but instead veered into a walkway that ran between two buildings and connected with an alley that ran parallel to the street.

He hurried to the back-door kitchen entrance of the Chez Louis.

The dark alley cloaked him in its shadows and in the

smell of aromatic cooking mingled with the stench of garbage overflowing from trash cans next to the kitchen door.

Tran hoped he was not late.

The call had come from the local cell leader. His instructions had come directly from Captain Quang. He had been ordered to assemble a team of gunmen.

Tran had worked with Chinh and Tho before, though he was only nineteen years old, a year older than his two companions. His street gang was feared even by the other gangs of youths that ran loose in the cities, those who had avoided school and military conscription one way or another. They made their living extorting money from small shopkeepers, threatening murder or to burn the businesses down if they were not paid. There was also good money in selling drugs to the whores and their G.I. customers in the Cholon District, a hotly contested turf among the street gangs. But again the cunning and brutality of Vo Tran and those who ran with him had secured their share of that illicit trade.

The Saigon police, under whose jurisdiction the gangs' activities fell, had their hands full with major crimes, usually involving the Communist cells, and so did not focus much attention on the gangs, often not realizing that the two were related.

Tran often sold the services of his gang to the cell of the People's Army to which he belonged. He considered himself shrewd for realizing that street crime could take one only so far. He felt it in his own best interests to belong to and serve the interests of the Vietcong.

Such as he was doing tonight.

He reached the back door of the restaurant and hovered there for a moment, peering in.

The kitchen was huge, well lighted, busy. Closest to

him were two men standing at a sink piled high with dishes, working busily with soap suds up to their elbows. Beyond them, chefs prepared the meals at long tables. Tuxedoed waiters sped smoothly past each other with trays of food, in and out of a set of swinging doors.

Tran was improvising. He had been given only a sketchy description of the American G.I. and the woman he was with. He was torn, standing there, between acting quickly and not knowing just what to do.

A busboy pushed a cart stacked high with dirty dishes and silverware through the set of swinging doors. He wheeled the cart over to the dishwashers standing just inside the screen door.

The busboy turned from having parked the cart next to the sink.

"You," Tran called under his breath.

The busboy heard, turned, and came over to stare out through the screen at Tran.

"Go away. You'll find no handouts here. Whatever's left that's worth eating when we close goes home with the chefs and the maître d'."

He started to turn away.

"That's not it." Tran summoned him back. "I've got a trishaw out front. He paid me some to wait for him, but he and his woman have been here a long time and—"

"So what is that to me." The busboy sneered. "Go away before you get me in trouble."

Tran extended a dong note. "The fare will be a good one if he is still inside with his date and I do take them back. But I have had American fares cheat me before. All I need to know is if he is in there."

Tran passed on the sketchy description he'd been given of the G.I., and the woman he would be dining with.

The busboy nudged the screendoor with his arm just

enough to reach out and snatch the money from Tran's fingers.

"They're in there, but it looked to me like they were preparing to leave," he said.

But he was already speaking to Tran's backside.

Tran bolted down the alley on his way back to the Citröen.

Tho and Chinh would do the actual killing. And the good thing for Tran was that he did not need to pay them in cash. They were doing it for heroin, for the drugs so many in the gangs were doing. The foolish ones, thought Tran. The expendable ones, like Chinh and Tho.

He had been ordered to see that the American did not leave the restaurant alive.

There was still time.

The order would be carried out.

Lieutenant Xong looked up from the paperwork spread out before him on his desk as the two ARVN regulars escorted Pham into the trailer that served as a joint office for Xong and Major Dow.

The captured Vietcong looked haggard, worried, and disoriented.

"I am to be taken to Saigon in the morning," he said when he saw Xong. "Major Dow said there would be no more interrogation of me here. Where is Major Dow?"

"The major is not on duty at this hour," said Xong.

The fear in Pham's eyes started to grow. "What is this about?"

"Major Dow has instructed me to question you regarding a few minor specifics regarding Captain Quang's operations in this area."

"But Major Dow said—"

"Major Dow has changed his mind. This will not take long. You will not be here in the morning. Have no fear."

"What do you want of me?"

Xong stood behind his desk and started forward. He nodded to the soldiers.

"You men may leave us. Stand guard outside. See to it that we are not disturbed. That is a strict order."

The sentries nodded. They turned and left the trailer.

The fear in Pham's eyes became panic.

As Xong saw the sentries out, he unlatched the flap of the holster at his hip. He closed and locked the door behind the sentries. He turned as soon as he was alone with Pham, taking out his pistol.

Pham had started to turn, to blurt out some sort of plea to Xong. He never completed the act.

Xong brought the butt of the pistol down sharply against Pham's temple.

Pham emitted a sound that sounded like a baby's gurgle. His eyes rolled back in their sockets. His knees knocked together and he collapsed to the floor of the trailer, where he lay unconscious, curled up in a fetal ball.

Xong worked quickly.

He holstered his pistol and snapped the flap shut. He went to his desk and withdrew a set of handcuffs, a roll of duct tape, and a scissors.

He returned to Pham and yanked his arms behind his back to handcuff him. Then he cut a strip off the roll of duct tape. He pressed down the patch of tape across Pham's mouth. The tape adhered firmly. He cut off a longer strip and wrapped it around Pham's ankles, binding them together.

Next Xong undid the knotted length of rope Pham wore around his waist to hold up the black trousers of his soiled Vietcong uniform. He wound one end of the rope around

Pham's neck and knotted it securely. Then he bent, slipped his arms through the handcuffed man's arms, and lifted him to his feet. Xong's physical strength served him well now. With a rough shove, he navigated Pham to a standing position against the wall near his desk.

Pham's eyes opened. Dazed at first, they orbed into white balls of terror an instant later when he realized that something was terribly amiss. He began to struggle violently, but could do little more than shake himself back and forth and try to strike out with his elbows. This was wholly ineffective in stopping Xong from going about his business in a grim, workmanlike manner.

A bolt, originally designed to hang a light fixture from, extended from the wall near the ceiling above Pham's head. Xong wrapped his iron grip around Pham's throat, pinned him to the wall, and started lifting his slight frame off the floor while he tugged at the rope that he had looped over the wall hook.

Xong released Pham's throat and held on to the rope with both hands. He braced one foot against the wall.

He stood thus, patiently, while Pham strangled to death. This took about three minutes.

When Pham's struggles ceased entirely and the stink of his voided bowels filled the room, Xong knew he was dead. Pham's trousers were around his ankles. It was not a pretty sight.

Xong continued his work methodically and with an efficient economy of movement. He made a knot in the rope around the bolt in the wall. He tugged the duct tape from the dead man's mouth and ankles and removed the handcuffs. He wadded up the used tape and tossed it into a wastebasket. He returned the rest of the evidence to the desk.

He stepped back for a moment to examine his handi-
work, searching objectively for a flaw.

He found one.

He moved the chair from behind his desk and rested it
on its side beneath the bottoms of Pham's feet, which dangled several inches from the floor.

Xong stepped back and reappraised his work.

It looked as it was supposed to look, as if Pham had
stood on the chair, tied the rope around his own neck and
the bolt in the wall, and kicked away the chair beneath
him.

Satisfied, Xong crossed the trailer, unlocked the door,
and stepped outside.

The sentries posted there turned at his appearance.

"I will be at the kitchen having a bowl of rice," he told
them. "The prisoner is reading a transcript of his testimony.
Allow no one to enter. If I have not returned within ten
minutes, check in on him to make sure everything is all
right. I will return shortly."

"Yes, sir," the sentries chorused in unison, saluting
smartly.

They did not see Lieutenant Xong's smile as he walked
away from them.

Ann saw them first.

Gaines stood at the register, paying the bill, momentarily distracted from the scene around them.

Ann gave his sleeve a tug as the woman behind the
register was counting out his change.

He looked up, followed the line of her gaze, and eye-
balled a pair of young men whom he pedigreed instantly as
street toughs.

They had no business in Chez Louis.

They came down the three carpeted steps leading from

the entranceway toward the cash register. At the foot of those steps, several paces from where Gaines and Ann stood, the punks split away from each other. They wore leather jackets despite the humid warmth of the night outside, and they were each grabbing under their jackets for what Gaines knew was hardware.

Gaines very ungently placed the palm of his left hand against the center of Ann's back and shoved her away from him.

Ann plowed into a couple waiting to pay their tab, and the three of them toppled.

A part of Gaines's mind was analyzing the commotion as if it were in slow motion, measuring, calculating his every response in the scant seconds he had to react before the toughs started blowing holes in him.

They were fast, no doubt high on something, but they were nothing but two-bit street punks, after all, and he had been staying alive in jungle combat for what seemed like a lifetime.

He threw himself bodily at the nearest punk before the kid's pistol fully lined itself up for a shot at him.

The punk must have expected to walk right up and open up, Gaines thought at that instant. They might have thought he would run. They had not considered that an unarmed man would charge full tilt into a pair of pistols being drawn on him.

The other gunman was still in the process of realigning his sights on Gaines's moving figure.

Gaines slammed into the first punk. His left arm straightened and went out, knocking the pistol from the kid's grip. His other fist delivered a powerhouse drive that knocked the kid off his feet.

Gaines kept his eye on where the punk's pistol landed.

He dove for it as the other gunman loosed two rounds that came nowhere near Gaines.

Males' shouts and females' shrieks pierced the air, furniture overturning as everyone dived for cover.

Gaines palmed the butt of the dropped automatic and rolled over onto his side, bringing the pistol around to sight in on the other gunman just as the punk was beading up for another shot.

Gaines hammered off three rounds reflexively, placing them tightly in the punk's heart area.

The kid died on his feet, his innards belching out his back from exit wounds. He slammed back into a wall and sunk to the floor, leaving a smear like some surreal painting upon the elegant wallpaper.

Gaines started to get to his feet.

Ann yelled, "Scott, behind you!"

Gaines was on his feet, whirling toward the direction the other gunman had fallen. Gaines had thought he'd taken care of the punk, but he was wrong.

The gunmen came at him suddenly, screaming like a banshee, raising a steak knife, appropriated from a nearby table.

Gaines pushed the scream back down the bastard's throat with a well-placed round that blew away the rear of the attacker's skull in a halo of spurting blood and brains.

There was an abrupt stillness in the restaurant except for the scared gibbering of some men and women hugging the floor under the tables. The rest were still in shock from this bit of wartime savagery in what was supposed to be a sanctuary.

Ann was on her feet and coming to Gaines's side.

"Scott, are you all right?"

"Fine. How about you, kid?"

"Just scared out of my skin!"

"That's twice you saved my life. When you spotted those punks and just now. Damn. That right hasn't failed me yet. Must have been that liqueur after dinner. He turned and headed toward the doorway. "Be right back, Ann. Stay put."

People were starting to get to their feet, gasping and staring at the bodies and murmuring questions among themselves and of the management. Some who were starting to come unglued began a panicky shouting.

"Where are you going?" Ann called after him.

"There might be a wheelman waiting outside for these guys with a car," Gaines shouted over his shoulder. "I want to know what this is about and who sent them."

Gun in hand, he bolted into the Saigon night.

EIGHT

Vo Tran, seated behind the steering wheel of the Citröen parked across the street and halfway up the block from Chez Louis, heard faintly the pistol fire from inside the restaurant.

From this distance, the shooting could have been no more than a jubilant partygoer setting off a string of fire-crackers in any of the restaurants and bistros that lined this stretch of Duong Tu-Do.

But Tran knew what the sound was.

He kept the Citröen at an idle with the headlights turned off. He held a U.S. Army .45-caliber Thompson subma-chine gun across his lap.

He watched the entrance of Chez Louis, expecting to see Tho and Chinh come dashing out, at which time he would speed across to pick them up at the opposite curb and whisk them away.

He sat there waiting for what seemed like a very long time.

Something had gone wrong, he decided. He turned on the lights and started to pull away from the curb.

That's when the American, Gaines, emerged from the restaurant.

Tran saw Gaines slip away from the lighted, canopied front entrance. Tran picked up speed, steering with his left hand, the index finger of his right curling around the trigger of the Thompson. He did not lose sight of Gaines.

Gaines stood in shadow next to the entrance. He held a pistol. He looked to his left, then to his right just as the Citröen drew abreast of him.

The vehicle was gaining speed, traveling in the far lane past the restaurant. Pedestrians and bicyclists were scrambling to get out of the way of the oncoming car, some angrily yelling.

Tran was certain that the pistol the American held had belonged to either Tho or Chinh. He was equally certain that both of those men were dead.

He reached out of the car with the submachine gun, aiming at the American. He opened fire in one sustained, sweeping burst.

Gaines saw the snout of the Thompson pointing at him. He yelled "Get to the ground" as loud as he could, once in English, once in Vietnamese. Then he threw himself flat to the pavement in the splinter of time between eyeing the machine gun and Tran's opening fire with it.

Some bystanders heard the American's warnings. Some of them fell to the ground to avoid the gunfire. Some of them ran for the nearest cover.

Mingled with the stuttering gunfire came the shouts and screams of panic and pain as the sweeping stream of bullets sprayed the entire area where Gaines had been standing.

Tran lost sight of Gaines in the confusion, but he did see

a dozen or more bystanders spasming into shuddering death dances as bullets riddled them.

A vehicle parked in front of the restaurant suddenly exploded into a resounding fireball of destruction, hurtling smoke and debris in every direction.

By this time Tran was well past the American. He was leaning his arm well outside the window, triggering the Thompson along his backtrack now as a Citröen continued gaining speed.

He ceased firing, threw the machine gun onto the seat beside him, and returned his attention to driving.

Too late.

There came the unmistakable *thump!* of hard metal plowing into a human body. He kept the Citröen's accelerator to the floor, and the body was hurled aside like a child's discarded rag doll. Whoever he had run down was a blur in the far corner of the windshield.

He told himself he had to have gotten the American, because he had swept the area with such thorough fire. It was too bad about the others. It was too bad about Tho and Chinh. But the American was dead, and all Tran could think about now was getting away.

Tran glanced into his rearview mirror, and all he could see was billowing smoke in front of Chez Louis where the car had been blown up, clearing the street of pedestrians and traffic. Then he saw a flicker of movement and what looked like a human form.

He was somehow certain, as certain as he had been that Tho and Chinh were dead, that the erect figure he saw striding into the center of the street in front of Chez Louis could be none other than Lieutenant Scott Gaines.

The figure raised both arms, assuming a two-handed firing stance.

Tran whipped his head back down to gauge his distance

from a corner where he could turn and escape. *I'm not going to make it!* The thought raced through his tumbling senses.

He did not hear the pistol shot.

He did hear the *blam!* of one of the rear tires catching the bullet. The Citröen swerved wildly. Tran lost control. The car leaped to the curb, and he slammed on the brakes.

The world reeled around Tran as the car slammed onto its side and skidded, leaving a trail of sparks, along the sidewalk pavement before ramming powerfully against some immovable obstacle.

Tran came to his senses in an awkward, twisted position. He felt something warm and wet coating one side of his face. He did not feel pain. He could see more than feel his body responding to his mental commands. He was in shock. He would feel pain later. Now it didn't matter.

Escape.

He smelled gasoline.

He scrambled around to extricate himself from the Citröen, now resting on its side.

Gaines! he thought. *I must get away from the American!*

The spilling, spreading gasoline from the ruptured tank had engulfed the Citröen's overheated engine.

Vo Tran never heard the explosion that ended his life.

It took some time and some doing for Gaines and Ann Bradley to make it back to Lai Khe that evening.

The Saigon police and the military police of the ARVN and the U.S. Army descended on Chez Louis with a vengeance. Each branch wanted to hear a full retelling of what had happened, not only from Gaines but from Ann and other eyewitnesses. This went on for quite a while, until jurisdiction problems were ironed out. By then it was well past midnight.

Miraculously, no one inside the restaurant had taken any of the errant rounds loosed by the hitmen.

The body count outside, however, was nine: four women, three men, and two children.

The consensus among the investigative personnel on the scene was that it was a random terrorist act against personnel of the U.S. military. Such attacks were common in Saigon.

Gaines wasn't so sure about that conclusion, but he kept his mouth shut on the subject.

He got the feeling the Saigon cops actually appreciated the elimination of three more troublemakers from the crime scene of their city. He managed to learn that the pair he'd greased inside the restaurant were members of a street gang.

Ann held up throughout the whole episode like the top-notch soldier Gaines knew her to be.

They'd been choppered back to the Lai Khe base after it was finally over.

In the chopper, dark except for the cockpit lights, they sat side by side on a bench attached to the fuselage, and in the darkness she entwined her fingers with his.

Gaines didn't mind at all.

They held hands like that all the way back to the base—like school kids on a date, thought Gaines—neither of them feeling compelled to communicate with spoken words.

The meeting at 0900 hours the following morning in Captain Carter's bunker was not as cordial as the debriefing following the destruction of the VC command complex.

Present were Carter; Gaines and his men, including Bok Van Tu; the ARVN officer, Major Dow, and a Lieutenant

Xong, whom Gaines had heard Dow refer to the day before as one of his best men.

After introducing Xong, Major Dow delivered Gaines a tight smile and a curt nod.

"I was most distressed to hear of the assault on you last night in Saigon, Lieutenant, and most pleased to hear of your good luck in dealing with your assailants."

"When the lieutenant starts dropping 'em," Hidalgo injected, "luck's got nothing to do with it."

"The only thing I didn't like about the way things turned out was that we lost any leads as to who sent those jerks after me," said Gaines. "But I'm more interested in your dead man. Let's talk about that guy Pham."

"I've briefed Lieutenant Gaines and his men on what you told me earlier today," Carter told Dow, "about Pham hanging himself last night."

"Most unfortunate." Dow nodded, then shrugged delicately. "They do not treat prisoners kindly in Saigon even if the prisoner is willing to cooperate, as Pham was. He must have known this. He expressed this fear to Lieutenant Xong."

Gaines looked at Xong. "Yet you left him alone?"

"He was safe enough, or so I thought," Xong said, avoiding Gaines's eyes. "I was gone for less than half an hour. The fault is mine. I accept the blame. I should have foreseen that in Pham's condition, he might go so far as suicide."

"You think it could have been that VC reprisal you were talking about yesterday?" DeLuca asked Dow.

Dow shook his head. "The sentries placed at the only entrance to that trailer, while Lieutenant Xong was away, have my full trust."

Hidalgo made no attempt to conceal his appraisal of

Lieutenant Xong. "Are you sure you're trusting the right people, man?"

Xong stared at the earthen floor of the bunker as if he had not heard.

"Enough of that, Private," Gaines reprimanded Hidalgo sharply. Then he said to Dow, "I remember you also saying you were going to assign Lieutenant Xong here to investigate those thefts of supplies and ammunition we've been having trouble with, the possibility that there might be a spy involved. We were talking about a full investigation."

"Lieutenant Xong," Dow prompted his junior officer.

Xong made eye contact with Gaines this time. "I regret to report that there have been no leads thus far."

"I've got a hunch that thievery is just the tip of something bigger," said Gaines, "and it's going to blow up in our face if we don't get serious about this."

"We are most serious about it, believe me," said Xong. "There is one bit of interesting information that Lieutenant Xong did unearth in his investigation. Lieutenant?"

"There are whispers we have picked up from among the peasants that indicate Captain Quang somehow managed to escape the destruction of his command base yesterday, although most of his force, including his own son, were killed."

"Is that all we have at this point?" asked Gaines. "No more than whispers?"

"I would be willing to place a wager that the rumors are true," said Dow.

"Keep pursuing that angle, then," Carter suggested. "It's no secret, Major Dow, that the ranks of the ARVN are riddled with Communist sympathizers."

"I assure you, my command is quite different," Dow said, bristling. "However, we shall leave no stone unturned. Come, Lieutenant Xong. Good day, gentlemen."

The Viet officers left the bunker stiffly and without further comment.

"What do you think, Tu?" asked Gaines. "Do you trust them?"

The Viet scout had stood off in a corner, but Gaines knew he had missed nothing of the exchange with the ARVN officers. Tu stepped forward.

"I do not trust them. I am not certain about Major Dow, but in my heart I know Lieutenant Xong is not one of us, is not on our side."

"That ain't exactly native intuition," DeLuca chided his Viet buddy with a grin.

Hidalgo nodded. "That son of a bitch Xong is slipperier than a bucket of worms."

Carter stood stroking his chin thoughtfully, eyeing the archway through which Dow and Xong had exited the bunker.

"There are plenty of good, dedicated ARVN soldiers," he said. "I'm just not so sure those two are among them. I'll get our people and ARVN Internal Affairs to look into it."

"That will have to do for now," said Gaines with no enthusiasm. He looked at the scout. "Tu, I think it would be a good idea for you to head on your own into Saigon and see what kind of information you can pick up on the streets."

"As you wish, Lieutenant," Tu said in his stilted, precise speech.

"Just don't get that skinny slope ass of yours shot off." Hidalgo grunted. "Get yourself greased, and I go back to being low man on the totem pole."

"It is where you belong, whitebread," Tu fired back with his famous grin. "Lieutenant, do you wish me to inquire regarding the assault on you and Nurse Bradley last night?"

Gaines nodded. "And see if you can substantiate the rumors Major Dow mentioned on Captain Quang escaping when we blew up those tunnels."

DeLuca's brow furrowed. "Do you think Quang had anything to do with the attack on you and Ann?"

"If he is alive, and if he lost a son," said Carter, "then Quang might figure he had a hell of a good reason for taking you out personally, Lieutenant."

"I didn't think it was a random shooting from the first," Gaines finally got around to telling them. "It was too well executed. They knew exactly where to find me, and they didn't waste any time getting down to business."

Carter frowned. "That would mean our spy supplied them with the information that you'd be at that restaurant."

Tu said, "If Captain Quang is alive . . . If a man like that declares a vendetta, it can only be a fight to the death."

"Sounds okay to me," Gaines growled. "You just hit your best two or three spots for picking up information," he instructed Tu. "Find out what you can as fast as you can and get back here with it in one piece before dark. We'll take care of the rest."

NINE

Even most of the civilians of the hamlets bordering the long-abandoned rubber plantation thought the old store-houses to be uninhabited.

Quang spent the day in the dingy, stifling heat of one of the structures, enveloped in a musty stench of jungle rot.

They wandered in one at a time throughout the middle part of the day so as not to draw attention to themselves.

There were nine of them, ten including Quang. Two were women.

Their leader was a young man in his early twenties named Vien.

Quang had dismissed the diggers early that morning, while the jungle was still shrouded in gloom. Their job was done, and they had done it well. The diggers were those committed to the cause enough to volunteer their time and effort.

But these, thought Quang, these were the ones whose eyes glistened with an intensity of purpose and a willingness to risk everything, even their lives, for the cause.

These were the killers.

During the night, Quang had received word of the failed assassination attempt on Scott Gaines and of the successful disposal of the matter of Pham the informer.

He had traveled to this rendezvous point alone and risked a few hours of sleep. He awoke some hours later to daylight and the slightest sounds of somone approaching.

He had been ready in the loft, crouched with his pistol ready, when the figure moved into view below him.

There was just a suggestion of daylight, dirty orange illumination filtered through vine-covered, grime-covered windows in the ceiling near the far end of the storehouse.

Quang could not be certain. "Stop right there," he commanded. "Turn very slowly."

The man did as he was told.

Quang recognized Vien. He lowered the pistol and climbed down the ladder to join him.

When the full crew arrived, Vien explained briefly to them that Captain Quang was in full command of this mission.

Quang then led them to the crates he had ordered brought here during the night.

Quang could hear Vien's people gasp as one when he pulled back the tops of the wooden crates and revealed the weaponry: AK-47s, an abundant supply of ammunition, and grenades.

Quang stepped back as the VC fighters armed themselves, each collecting as much ammunition and grenades as they could carry, strapping bandoliers across their chests.

The fighters were smiling widely, chattering excitedly to each other.

"I should not wish to dampen your enthusiasm," Quang snapped with a touch of sarcasm, "but I hope Vien has told you that this could be a suicide mission."

The chattering ceased.

"I told them," said Vien. "I also told them what you told me when you contacted me last night: that our plan may be audacious enough that we will sustain only a minimum of losses."

"It is up to you," Quang told the group of them. "My son Tsing worked this out carefully. I am following his plans. They shall serve us well tonight." He withdrew a folded piece of paper and spread it out on a nearby barrel. "This is a map of the compound at Lai Khe. The Americans will never expect what we are about to do. We will attack in the early-morning hours. You must memorize the map and my instructions. We want to get in and out and do as much damage and kill as many American soldiers as we possibly can."

One American in particular, Quang thought as he spoke. He would see to it before they attacked that he would know where to find Lieutenant Scott Gaines.

Quang intended to kill Gaines personally.

Ann Bradley and Captain Phil Stevens left Lai Khe at 0800 that morning, taking Highway 13 south for several kilometers before on the secondary dirt road that cut due west into the jungle in the direction of Hoa Phu.

The day was already stiflingly hot despite an ominous, low cloud ceiling. Thunder rumbled in the distance.

No rain. Humidity in the upper nineties. Ann knew that the weather might stay like this for days.

Stevens drove the jeep. The canvas roof was up, but the sides were open. On the highway the breeze whipping through the jeep had helped dry the perspiration that soiled

their fatigues and made the extreme mugginess somewhat
more tolerable.

The road dipped and wound its way through the foothills. It was in a severe state of disrepair because of recent
heavy rains, and the going was slow and bumpy.

Steven cursed under his breath. He fought the bucking
steering wheel, dodging ruts and potholes when he could.

The jeep seemed to crawl along in third gear, and the
farther they traveled from the main highway behind them,
the rougher the road became.

Ann held on to the frame of the jeep to keep from being
spilled out onto the roadside. She watched the road ahead,
paying particular attention to the thick vegetation to either
side. From anywhere along here, she knew, trouble could
pounce upon them.

They passed a U.S patrol and, in front of a hut plastered
with Coca Cola and Lucky Strike signs, a cluster of G.I.s
taking five. They saw a convoy of four vehicles carrying
infantrymen of the Bloody Red One—jeep, tarp-covered
transport, and two open trucks.

Stevens was cursing with every pull of the steering
wheel. Ann glanced his way, a part of her wanting to ignore his evident frustration and anger. Another part of her
could not suppress the concern for him she had felt growing.

He was a not unhandsome man of thirty-three, medium-
sized, sandy-haired. But there were discolored pouches
under his eyes, and she could detect the scent of whiskey
about him.

They were less than a half-kilometer from Hoa Phu.
Except for Stevens's cussing of the road, they had not spoken since leaving Highway 13.

"I know you outrank me, Phil," she said at last, "but I

would be remiss were I not to point out that you look like shit and you smell like a distillery."

He chuckled, a chuckle with the chill of bitterness and weariness to it. "Interesting mental image, shit in a distillery. But thanks for the thought, Ann. Okay, I'll cool down. Sorry, and thanks for caring."

"It would have been all right with me not to have made this trip today," she said in a softer tone. "If you're not feeling up to it—"

"Don't even say that," he said in a stronger tone. "There are people waiting for us in this village up ahead who have walked in from miles around, sick people who are counting on us. I want to help those people. Guess my nerves are just a little on the frayed side."

"I think it does you good to get away from the base like this, to pull back from that pressure."

He chuckled again. This time the sound was warmer, more natural.

"Right as usual, Lieutenant Bradley. I remember now that that's another reason I volunteered for this. You volunteered, and we were lovers at the time."

"Phil, please—" she started to protest.

He broke into one of his warm smiles that she liked so much and he waved a hand good-naturedly.

"Don't worry, Ann. I've got the picture about you and Scott Gaines. I'm glad we're just friends. That's changed, but nothing else has. I'm glad neither one of us is doing this solo, especially since it's our own time."

She moved her eyes from him, back to the road ahead where it curved before its approach to the village.

"I dig your company too, Captain." After their affair of the heart, it had become a point of some humor between them to address each other formally. *Crazy, mixed up world*, she thought for the millionth time since coming to

Vietnam. She said, "You're a fine, gentle person, Phil. We'll get out of this war in one piece."

She was counting on losing herself in the concerns of those she was coming to treat to help her forget the violence and death she had witnessed during the attempt on Gaines's life the night before in Saigon.

That shooting had become highly classified before they had even touched down in that chopper after the night flight back to the base.

The matter would be mulled over by Scott and his team and others immediately concerned, Scott had told her, but in case it was tied in with something bigger as he suspected, he wanted the lid kept on it, and so, apparently, did Captain Carter.

She had taken a Valium the night before, which had helped her get to sleep but had not brought on the deep sleep that rejuvenates the body and spirit.

But she was feeling energized as they were almost at the village.

"I just want you to know," Stevens said, "that I think Scott Gaines is one hell of a good man."

"He and I are—"

"I know, just friends. It doesn't matter. That's all I want to be, Ann. Just friends. I'll settle for that any day, and I'll be there anytime you need me."

"I know that, Phil. Thanks, and ditto."

He steered the jeep into the curve that would bring them into sight of the village.

"Well, all right, then," he said. "Let's get to work."

Hoa Phu nestled in a valley formed by gradually sloping, forested hills that climbed to rocky ridges. These ridges provided Noh and his bandit gang a perfect vantage point.

The bandit chief stood, resting his elbows on a boulder to steady his field of vision, and panned the view from this high ground. Ky stood at his side, as always, and behind him the other bandits squatted against the rocks or sat upon the pebbly ground, making last-minute checks of their weaponry and ammunition.

The village consisted solely of about a dozen bamboo-and-mud huts. These were single-room structures. Most of them had a lean-to shack attached that served as a kitchen.

There were none of the primitive shops or restaurants that occasionally might be found in such a village. The villagers of Hoa Phu were peasant farmers.

The farmers raised crops like melons, grapefruit, and cashew nuts. There was a communal corral adjacent to one of the melon patches. Buffalo lazed in the corral.

Normally, on market day Hoa Phu would be busy, the wide dirt streets running between the huts lined with stalls. But today only an occasional villager could be seen moving about, while pigs and poultry roamed freely.

Slight sounds carried up to the bandits' position because of the low clouds: animal sounds, snippets of conversation that could not be made out. Lazy sounds. This was a lazy life.

But yes—Noh nodded to himself—ripe for the picking, as Ky had said last night.

Noh moved his binoculars to where the road leading through the village appeared from a cut in the hills, a quarter of a kilometer away.

A U.S. Army jeep moved into view. Its engine noise had been muffled by the terrain and foliage but now carried uphill clearly as it proceeded into the center of the village and stopped. Two American soldiers, a man and a woman, stepped from the jeep. They wore fatigues. They did not wear sidearms, Noh noted, and no rifles were visible.

They were greeted by the village headman, who stood before a small group of villagers.

The Americans commenced unloading boxes from the jeep. The boxes looked to be filled with bottles and medical supplies, though Noh could not be sure.

"What is this?" Ky said, lowering his binoculars from his eyes. "A complication?"

"Hardly that," said Noh. "American medical personnel, most likely from Lai Khe, here to dispense drugs and treatment to those of the village."

Ky's eyes gleamed. "Medical supplies would fetch a good price on the black market. The Vietcong would pay well."

"They shall pay well." Noh nodded. "Our attack on the village when the American convoy passes through could not be better timed." He panned the binoculars toward the cut in the hills through which the jeep had appeared.

"Do you think something has gone wrong?" said Ky. "The Americans will not come this way?"

"They are late, but they will come, and soon. I had best be on my way."

Noh went to the rusty, bent bicycle leaning against the trunk of a tree. There was a wire basket in front attached to the handlebars. The basket appeared to hold no more than folded-up clothes, but beneath the clothes was an American-made .45 automatic and a hand grenade.

Noh handed his binoculars to Ky. He picked up the bike and put the frame over one shoulder.

"Have the men split up and position themselves as we discussed," he said. "At first sight of the convoy, I will pedal into the village and it will begin."

Ky licked his lips. "We will be ready."

Noh turned and began walking away. He started at an angle that would take him down the slope, allowing him to remain out of sight of anyone in the village. He was headed for a point on the road several hundred meters beyond the far side of the cluster of huts.

He had not gone far when the noise of an approaching helicopter sent him and the men he had left behind scurrying for cover.

They managed to conceal themselves a fraction of an instant before the Huey gunship thundered by at little more than treetop level.

Noh and his men cautiously straightened and reappeared after the sounds had died away.

Noh lifted his arm in a short farewell wave to Ky and the others. He could feel his pulse racing in anticipation of what was to come.

He resumed walking downslope, toward the road.

The convoy would come soon.

Then the killing could begin.

Somewhere in the distance, thunder rumbled ominously.

TEN

Sergeant E-5 Tom Hines followed with his eyes the Huey gunship buzzing by overhead on routine patrol. Then he brought his gaze groundward and frowned.

Lieutenant Bonham stood engaged in the same inane, flirtatious conversation with the Viet store clerk.

Hines, a chocolate-hued man of medium size whose crisply starched fatigues belied the wilting humidity, cursed under his breath.

Hines was from South Carolina. He had lied about his age and gotten into the Army just in time to join the bloody mop-up of the Philippines in the final days of WWII. He'd fought his way through Korea and had emerged with the Congressional Medal of Honor, enough citations to paper a good-size wall, and the sure knowledge that a man of his race could go a hell of a lot further, as far as pay and advancement were concerned, inside the military than out.

And so here he was, he told himself. Top kick of a

company of infantry, with the trust of every man invested squarely on his shoulders.

The convoy had stopped at the modest little store at Bonham's orders, and they'd been here for close to a half hour.

The men lounged around the troop carriers and the tarp-covered truck that contained rations and supplies for the Special Forces base camp deep in the highlands beyond Hoa Phu.

Hines had established a defense perimeter and tried to bite his tongue, holding back his opinion of this shavetail punk first louie. But enough was enough.

"Load up," he ordered his men. "We're getting ready to pull out."

The men began climbing aboard the truck.

Hines heard mutterings, and he couldn't blame them. He knew just how they felt.

Bonham looked around from the girl as Hines approached. The first lieutenant was pressed against the young woman and they leaned on a wall, engaged in conversation.

She was a looker, Hines thought to himself, despite her obvious lack of taste in men. Vietnamese women were said to be the most beautiful in the Orient, and from what he'd seen, he was inclined to agree, though he had never sampled the charms of a Viet woman.

He did not frequent the bars and cathouses. He was married to a woman he loved, who was waiting for him back in the World with their two daughters.

"What is it, Sergeant?"

"I've ordered the men to load up, sir. Told 'em we're moving out."

Bonham had been so engrossed in his flirtations that he

had not even noticed. Disapproval laced his response.

"Well, have them unload. I give the orders, Top. We're not done here."

"You're done here," said Hines, unruffled. "The only reason we made this stop at all was—"

"The men needed a rest," the lieutenant interrupted defensively.

"They've had their rest," said Hines. "You'll have to carry on your love life on your own time, sir." He spoke as if the girl were not present.

Her eyes were appraising Bonham to see how he would handle himself.

"Sergeant—" he started to say, trying to regain command of this confrontation.

He did not succeed.

"Lieutenant," said Hines, making the word sound like an insult. He pitched his voice low enough not to be overheard by the men in the trucks, but his tone was rock hard. "I volunteered for this mission. With my rank I could be sitting behind a desk in an air-conditioned office."

"Then why did you come, Sergeant?"

Hines cocked his head to indicate the men in the trucks without breaking steely eyeball contact with Bonham.

"These are my men," he snapped. "They're good men. Most of them aren't much more than boys. I wasn't about to put their safety in the hands of a shavetail with no combat experience. Since you ask, sir," he tacked on with no attempt to veil the contempt he felt for the man he was speaking to.

"Well, since you did come along, Sergeant, I'd advise you to follow orders from your superior officer and—"

"Our mission is to get these supplies to that base camp," Hines said as if Bonham had not spoken. "Our responsibility is to get our men back to Lai Khe before nightfall. And it sure as hell isn't a good idea to stand still in one place as long as we have. Charlie will get wind that we're here, and we'll have a firefight on our hands before we know it."

"I hardly think so, Top. You saw that chopper that just flew by. This region is—"

"Secured, yeah. Look, Lieutenant, I've seen too many boys shipped home in body bags because some hotshot officer didn't pay attention to his noncom. Son, I was dodging bullets before you were peeing in your first set of diapers. We're moving out. You can come with us, or you can stay here acourtin' and we'll pick you up on our way back."

"Sergeant, your insubordination will be duly noted when we get back to Lai Khe."

"Let's just worry about making it back. Oh, and something else, Lieutenant. Those boys I was talking about, the ones who were bodybagged home because of their hotshot officers . . ." Hines paused for effect, then finished. "Their hotshot officers were bodybagged right along with them." He looked at the young woman for the first time and nodded. "Miss." Then he turned and strode back toward the jeep.

There was a slight exchange between Bonham and the girl, then Hines could hear the lieutenant tagging along behind him.

The drivers started up the engines.

Thi Sang was one of the more than one million North Vietnamese who had fled south across the 17th Parallel in 1954 after the French defeat.

The North had become a Communist dictatorship. The South became the Republic of Vietnam.

There were friends, some relatives, who had chosen to stay behind, who had reasoned that Communist rule would not be so bad.

Sang had never heard from them again after coming south.

Thi Sang was the village headman of Hoa Phu. He liked Americans. He understood that war breeds madness in all men who fight it, no matter their nationality or beliefs. But his experiences with Americans had led him to the understanding that they were by nature a brash, perhaps overloud, but basically friendly people.

He especially liked Phil Stevens and Ann Bradley, who regularly came to his village to dispense medical assistance.

Thi understood racism. He knew his people were called "slopes" and "gooks" and were looked down upon by many Americans serving in Vietnam. But he also knew that such attitudes often are born of fear.

But Phil and Ann were Americans at their best, in Sang's estimation. They were brave—their presence in his village proved that—and they were generous. They had even done their best to learn snatches of the local dialect, something few Americans seemed interested in doing.

Sang stood to the side and watched the two lines moving slowly past the folding tables Ann and Phil had set up.

The Americans spoke with each person. At times Sang was called on to interpret.

Thunder rumbled.

Sang hoped it would not rain on these people doing their good work. But if rain did come, they could find shelter in his hut, the largest in the village.

He heard a faint rumbling and at first thought it was

more thunder. Then, through the cut in the hills, he saw a U.S. Army convoy.

Ann and Phil looked up but continued their work.

The vehicles came on. A jeep was followed by a truck. The back of the truck was covered by a tarp, and the end-flaps closed. A pair of troop carriers followed, young men in the backs seated with their weapons aimed skyward.

Something caught Sang's eye. He frowned when he saw the bicyclist, whom he did not recognize.

Hines was riding shotgun in the comm jeep, his M-16 on lock and load and his eyes trying to watch everything at once.

Bonham rode in the backseat of the jeep. He had not spoken since back at the roadside store, but he wore an aura of fuming anger.

Not that Hines gave a good goddamn. It was time to deal with the lieutenant through proper channels before Bonham got some good man killed or before some good man got in a world of trouble for fragging Bonham's ass.

Hines forgot all about that now, his eyes narrowing on the bicyclist, now no more than several dozen yards away. Cold chills traced their way up and down his spine.

"Stop," he said quietly to Hogarth.

The driver applied the brakes.

Bonham leaned forward, snarling irritably, his head between Hines and Hogarth.

"Why are we slowing down?"

Hines pointed. "That bicyclist."

"What about him?"

"Something's wrong."

"What the fuck bug do you have up your ass now, Sergeant?" Bonham barked. "Keep going, driver. I'm the one giving the orders. What's wrong with that bicyclist?" he demanded of Hines.

Hogarth did not pick up speed as ordered. His eyes were on Hines.

Hines said, "Where the hell is that guy going? Where's he coming from? I know this country. There are bicycles all over Saigon and the larger towns, but not out here. Stop the jeep," he snarled at Hogarth.

"You take your orders from me,' Bonham snapped. "Keep going."

Hogarth kept the jeep coasting, his eyes on Hines.

Hines said, "If I'm right, he'll go for us, knock out our communications."

"That's crazy," Bonham snapped.

The bicyclist was abreast of them now. He reached under the stash of clothes in the basket and withdrew a grenade. He pulled the pin with his teeth and pitched it at the open jeep.

Hines saw it coming. He had time to snarl over his shoulder, "Damn your soul to hell, Bonham."

Then he threw himself from the jeep. He hit the ground smoothly with one shoulder and went into a combat roll, then propelled himself to his feet.

The grenade went off seconds later.

The vehicle skidded onto its side, a smoking, twisting wreck that Hogarth or Bonham could never have survived.

There were screams and shouts from the periphery. Automatic fire could be heard, the distinctive crackle of AK-47s. The windshields of one of the trucks disintegrated, the driver and another soldier blown apart by slashing bullets and shards of glass.

Men were piling out of the trucks. Some of them tumbled under the enemy fire before they could reach cover.

"*Damn* you to hell, Bonham," Hines snarled again.

He heard firing from his left. He whipped his M-16 around. But before that maneuver could be completed, he saw the trio of men who had been firing on the trucks. They were already aiming their weapons on him.

The thought that he would never see his wife and children again was Tom Hines's final thought.

Then the hail of machine-gun fire downed him.

And the killing continued around his fallen body.

ELEVEN

The little girl was trying very hard to be brave. Her eyes were squeezed shut and her lips quivered, but she held out her arm for Ann to work on. The girl's other arm was held reassuringly by her mother, who stood at her side.

Ann idly glanced over the girl's shoulder and saw the bicyclist at about the same time a convoy of U.S. Army trucks came rumbling into the village from the direction of Lai Khe.

She noticed that Thi Sang had started walking to intercept the bicyclist.

Ann went back to bandaging the girl's infection, Phil seated at the table beside her.

At that moment, a quiet day in Hoa Phu erupted into unthinkable, nightmarish horror.

Ann heard the grenade go off with a peculiarly muted sound. She whipped her head around to see smoke pouring out of the convoy's lead jeep. The jeep wobbled about aimlessly before it plowed into a hut, collapsing it.

"Aw, *shit*," she heard Phil rasp.

A man—a black sergeant, she could see—was pulling himself up from the ground, swinging up his rifle.

The shouts of attacking men filled the air, then were buried beneath the chattering of AK-47s from several angles at once.

Concealed gunners raked the trucks. Men died crying out, their bodies blown apart before they could return fire.

She saw the black sergeant receive a row of bullets across his chest that pulped him apart at the middle, blowing bloody chunks everywhere.

She and Stevens threw themselves to the ground.

Before they could say or do anything, she saw the man who had been riding the bicycle.

He had picked up an AK-47 of his own and emerged from behind the headman's hut.

She knew what he was about to do.

All about them were screaming, shouting civilians. Adults herded children to safety, everyone running for their lives.

Ann thought of the weapons in their jeep, several dozen feet away. Phil had brought a .45 automatic; she an M-16. She had qualified with both. Her father had taught her how to shoot before she'd ever left home.

"We've got to get to the jeep!" she told Phil over the crackle of weapons.

Stevens looks dazed, in shock. "Uh, right," he muttered.

They scrambled for the jeep.

Random bullets whistling everywhere around them, they reached the jeep, gained the far side of it for cover.

Ann reached in, handed Stevens his holstered .45, and grabbed her rifle. She tried not to look at what happened next, but she could not avoid it.

The bicyclist opened fire. He stood there with a calculated coldness, and his body rocked to the recoil of the flaming AK-47 in his fists.

The concentrated burst blew apart Thi Sang, the little girl, and her mother just as they were momentarily grouped in the doorway of the headman's hut. The three people were tossed about in awful death jigs as the hail of projectiles sprayed the front of the hut with bursting blood.

Ann cried out, a wail of disbelief and abhorrence and denial. Then she was screaming her rage, and her body was rocking under the steady hammering of the M-16.

The bicyclist dodged behind the hut. The wall where he had been standing pulverized into flying chunks, but none of the bullets struck him.

Phil held his pistol in a two-handed grip, aiming across the hood of the jeep as Ann was, but he did not fire. He swung frightened eyes on her.

"Let's get the hell out of here," he said, starting around her toward the driver's seat.

The gunfire had tapered off. There seemed to be no more resistance from the direction of the convoy.

"Those aren't VC," said Ann, standing her ground. "These are bandits, Phil."

"I don't give a fuck who they are," he snapped. "This isn't our fight. We're not even supposed to be here!" He spewed the words in a fevered panic. His face was white, beaded with sweat.

"Phil, don't be a coward. There are people here who need us."

"We won't go far," he said, climbing aboard the jeep. "We'll be back when the shooting's over. We're noncombatants, for chrissake, Ann. We—"

She crouched down behind the jeep and turned her attention to argue, to talk sense to him.

Projectiles whistled close overhead. Some pinged off the jeep's chassis and several more blew apart both tires on the other side of the vehicle.

She saw Stevens's reflexive hunch to the side, but before he could throw himself from the jeep, a bullet caught him high in the right side of the chest. The impact flung him head over heels from the jeep. He lay sprawled upon his back amid a small rising cloud of red dust.

Ann pulled the M-16 up and squeezed off a burst at two bandits running over to join the one behind the hut. They dodged to the ground behind cover.

She lost sight of them but knew she'd missed, that there were now three of them behind that hut no more than several yards away.

She stopped firing. Her eyes swept the village.

Some of the huts were already being torched.

A bandit was walking among the fallen American bodies, delivering a head shot to each one.

She rested the M-16 against the jeep. Keeping low, she rushed over to Stevens.

He was sitting. Much of his right upper chest area, including much of the shoulder, was palpitating, raw red-black shattered bone and flesh.

"Damn, the little fuckers got me," he groaned through teeth clenched against the pain. "Had it coming. I always was a lousy fucking coward. Damn!"

"Don't talk like that now, Phil," she told him. "We'll get out of here."

She peered over the hood of the jeep. No sign of the trio of bandits behind the hut.

"Don't bullshit a bullshitter, Ann," Stevens bit off. "I'm a doctor, remember. Only reason I'm not feeling it more is shock, and that's going to wear off any second, and when it does the pain will knock me out if I don't black out first from . . . loss of blood."

"Oh, Phil—"

He weakly lifted the pistol with his left hand. "I can . . . hold them . . . it's over here . . . Save yourself, Ann . . . Go, kid . . . go . . . and good luck with Gaines . . . he's a hell of a guy . . . Now, beat it . . ."

A trickle of blood worked its way from the corner of his mouth to run down his chin.

She hesitated for a second, not knowing what to do.

The shooting in the village had stopped. The only movement came from the crackling flames of burning huts.

Suddenly, the three bandits leaped from the jungle line no more than fifty feet from the near side of the jeep, having circled around from the rear of the hut.

"Run!" Stevens rasped at Ann with all the strength he could muster.

He raised his pistol at the bandits and opened fire.

Ky broke from the treeline with Noh and one of the other bandits. He saw the Americans, and a smile twisted his mouth into an ugly grimace. It was he who had walked among the fallen Americans back by the trucks, leaning over to deliver a head shot to each one of them.

Some of them had still been alive, and he'd enjoyed killing them the most, had enjoyed seeing them, hearing their screams, in the instant before he blew their brains upon the ground.

It was at those moments that all else faded away and he lived for vengeance upon these foreign invaders who had murdered his wife and four children and destroyed their farm with napalm.

Later could come the spoils of war. Killing Americans made him high, like some incredibly potent drug.

And here were two more!

He and the bandit at his side raised their AK-47s and would have mowed the Americans to pieces if Noh had not made a quick gesture for them not to fire.

"We want these Americans alive," said the bandit chief.

Ky acted as if he did not hear Noh's command. His hatred fueled his insanity.

"Americans must die!" he screamed in English. "Death to Americans!"

He fired a sustained burst that plopped the American man this way and that, with guts and blood billowing.

Noh said coolly, "I demand obedience, Ky. The others will learn from your example."

He turned his AK-47 on Ky and fired a three-round burst that kicked Ky off his feet and deposited him like so much discarded garbage.

Noh looked at the other man.

"Come with me. We must catch that woman. I want her alive."

"Yes, sir," the man said without a glance at Ky's remains.

"After her, then!"

They ran off in the direction taken by the American woman.

She knew they would catch her, but she could not stop running, could not give up.

She ran through the jungle. The loudest sound in her ears was her own breathing. Her heart slammed against her rib cage like a bass drum gone berserk. Perspiration dripped into her eyes.

A vine tripped her. She fell, dropping the rifle, breaking the fall with her arms. She picked herself up and, wiping the sweat from her eyes, retrieved the rifle and ran.

Images swirled through her brain: the horrors of the massacre, the atrocities she had witnessed, the death of a good man named Phil Stevens. All of these images drove her on.

Her feet tripped over another knotted growth of jungle vine. She fell forward, and again the force of the fall jolted the rifle from her hands. She tried to disengage her feet, but they were tangled in the vines.

Then they were upon her, slightly out of breath from the chase. They slowed when they saw her, then came forward to stand over her.

One of them smiled. Not a pleasant smile. He had a scarred and pockmarked face and eyes of brutality.

"Hello, American lady," he said in a rough accent. "Very nice to see you."

He nodded to the bandit with him, no more than a boy.

The boy stepped forward and swung the rifle butt to connect with the side of Ann Bradley's head.

Pain and stars in spreading blackness filled her as she slipped into unconsciousness.

Her last thought was a strange one: that she would never live to make love with Scott Gaines.

TWELVE

Bok Van Tu arrived by bus in downtown Saigon shortly after noon.

He began without delay his pursuit of leads "on the street," as Lieutenant Gaines had phrased it.

Gaines was one of the bravest fighters and best men the Kit Carson scout had ever known—Vietnamese, American, or otherwise.

For this reason, Tu's assignment to personally investigate the attack on Scott Gaines—and the rumors of Captain Quang's having survived the Tunnel Rat's destruction of his tunnels, and any possible link between these two threads—meant more to Tu than merely following orders from his American officers.

Gaines had saved Tu's life in combat only the week before.

Tu agreed with Gaines that the attack on Gaines and his date in the French restaurant was more than a random terrorist act. He welcomed the opportunity to take direct action that might in some way repay the American lieutenant.

It had been nearly two years since Tu's defection from the Vietcong, and it was something he had never regretted.

It had hardly been his capture alone that had brought about his defection. Most captured VC did not defect. But Tu had been of a high enough rank to be aware of things many among the ranks of the Vietcong did not know.

Tu had been early on swept up in the ideological Marxist movement, distressed at what he had perceived to be the corrupting influences on his country's government by the foreign powers that had so long seemed to control Vietnam's destiny.

After several years of fighting the Americans, however, Tu had seen the ways in which those who fought in and for the Vietcong were themselves being manipulated by forces he deemed far worse than American for the best interests of his country. He came to understand that he and those men and women he fought and died with were no more than pawns.

Reports of the way things were in the North after the Communists had come to power had trickled down to the South. Harsh martial law had been imposed. All dissent was eradicated through mass executions and fear.

In the South, Tu knew that atrocities committed by the Vietcong against the civilian population made any similar type of acts on the part of the Americans insignificant.

Tu was aware of the massacre at My Lai of civilians by a small unit of Americans, but he understood this to be the isolated exception that it was.

War bred madness in men, and no one was immune.

The difference was that the Vietcong committed atrocities that were coldblooded, well thought out, meant to spread terror and destabilize the country.

Tu did not want this for Vietnam.

A democratic form of government at least allowed the people the possibility of reform, of change from within, of rooting out the corruption.

Tu had come to think that if the Communists could be stopped, the killing could be stopped. That is what he wanted for his country. That is why he defected.

Tu himself knew of far too many young men, sons of his neighbors, friends and relatives, who had been conscripted into Vietnam's army and had fought and died on the field of combat. It was to honor their memory that he hoped in his small way to improve the image of his people in the eyes of the Americans by his example.

Tu did not trust Dow and Xong, the ARVN officers at Lai Khe. He hoped information he learned in Saigon this day would work against them if they were guilty of conspiring against the Americans. Tu was far prouder to fight with the likes of men like Scott Gaines, Frank DeLuca, and Johnny Hidalgo.

Before leaving the base, Tu had learned from Gaines the names of his assailants—Vo, Chinh, and Tho—and the fact that they were members of a youth gang in Saigon.

This had simplified things for him. He knew exactly where to go upon arriving in the city.

He knew Saigon as well as he knew the jungle, and Gaines had instructed him to return to the base before nightfall. Tu knew why.

If Captain Quang was alive, Gaines and his Tunnel Rats would want to go out hunting the Vietcong commander down as a matter of personal integrity—since it had been their responsibility to destroy Quang and his tunnels. Captain Carter would arrange their assignment to that end because Carter would understand, as Tu did, that it was as personal a cause for Gaines as it was for Quang.

The Kit Kat Club was on a side street of small businesses and shops. The club was owned by a boyhood friend of Tu's named Nguyen Quot.

The red-light district was not far from the bar. In fact, until Quot had bought the club, it had been a hangout for prostitutes and dope dealers even after the Army declared it off limits. When Quot bought the place, he immediately threw out the unsavory element and went about the slow process of establishing the club's respectability.

The last time Tu had spoken with his friend, however, Quot had explained that a new element was beginning to frequent the bar: members of one of the street gangs.

The club was nothing more than a square, low-cei-linged, tile-floored room, dimly illuminated even at mid-day. There was a bar along one wall, a scattering of tables around a dance floor, and a jukebox, now silent.

Quot sat on a stool behind the bar, leafing through a magazine. He looked up, and when he saw Tu seating himself at the bar, his bored expression turned into a wide smile.

"Well, my friend, this is a pleasant surprise. I did not expect to see you this day. What will be your pleasure?"

"A beer. It is good to see you, Nguyen."

As the bar owner reached for a bottle of Tu's regular brand of beer, Tu stole a glance down along the bar at three young men who could barely have been more than the legal drinking age.

They had been staring at him. They returned his glance

with snickers among them, saying things to each other that he could not hear.

Quot set the beer on the bar in front of Tu. He waved away the money Tu extended him.

"No, I will buy this one, my friend. It is a relief to have someone in here whose company I enjoy for a change."

Tu nodded in the direction of the young toughs. "Do they cause trouble?"

"Some. They have chased most of my customers away."

"Why don't you throw them out or call the police?"

"I threatened to do that last week."

"What happened?"

"They are gang members. They beat me. They said they would again if there is any more trouble, as they called it. They know that I alone am no match for them. They are no good. They should be in jail."

"Did you know the one called Vo Tran?"

Quot nodded. "He was the leader of this gang of thugs. He came in here all the time. He and the other two who were killed with him last night."

"Who will the leader of the gang be next?"

"They will fight, they will kill, amongst themselves for that power," said Quot.

"I want to find out who was responsible for sending Vo and that pair after those Americans in the restaurant last night," said Tu.

Quot's brow furrowed. "May I ask why you are involved in such things?"

"It is because I know the American they were after. His name is Lieutenant Scott Gaines. He is my friend. I work with him. I came here for information that will help him."

"If this American friend of yours killed three of this

gang," said Quot, "he is a friend of mine and I will do what I can to help."

"Do you know the name, Captain Quang?"

"Since yesterday I have known it. I overhead Vo and the others talking. This Captain Quang has placed a bounty on Lieutenant Gaines, and not just Vo's gang will try to collect it. Scott Gaines is a marked man as long as Captain Quang is alive."

Tu nodded to himself. "I was sure Quang was alive. I could feel it somehow. Do you know where he is?"

Quot shook his head and opened his mouth to respond, but he was interrupted when the toughs seated at the far end of the bar sidled over to stand in a semicircle around Tu's barstool.

Tu swiveled slowly around on the stool and sat with his back against the bar.

One of the toughs said, "You're asking too many questions. Who are you?"

"A man who asks too many questions."

"We heard you say the name Scott Gaines. We are looking for the American."

"So you can collect Captain Quang's reward?"

"Of course," the tough replied unflinchingly. "You will tell us where Gaines is."

"No," said Tu. "You will tell me where I may find Captain Quang."

The toughs snickered again.

"There are three of us and only one of you," the youth in the middle pointed out.

"There are two of us," Quot corrected from behind the bar.

The three gang members spread apart slightly and, as one, reached behind them and withdrew from back pockets of their slacks one folded knife each. The young hoodlums each flicked a wrist in unison and the knife blades appeared, long and menacing and glinting at Tu and Quot in the overhead lights.

"You will tell us what we want to know," snarled the one in the middle menacingly. "Where is the American, Scott Gaines?"

"You will tell me what I wish to know." Tu said in a very quiet voice.

Then he leaped from the stool almost faster than the eye could see, assuming a martial-arts stance, raising his arms with his right hand poised to strike, his left forearm defensively horizontal to his chest.

He waited another second until the trio of hoodlums facing him started to lunge forward together, then struck with a grunted shout.

He delivered a kung fu blow, a knuckle punch that connected with the center of the forehead of the one on his left. The hoodlum's eyes rolled back in his head and he collapsed, unconscious.

The hoodlum in the middle started to back away, but not quickly enough. Tu pivoted around with another shout and delivered a powerful hook kick to the tough's abdomen.

The hoodlum whoofed his air out and doubled over under force of the blow. He fell to the floor to lay upon his side, wretching, in a fetal ball.

The third hoodlum lifted his knife and started to charge at Tu until a well-aimed, full beer bottle hurled by Quot connected with the boy's forehead. The tough collapsed, unconscious.

Tu stepped over to stand above the wretching hoodlum. He brought the sole of one boot to the young man's throat and leaned on that leg ever so slightly.

The young man gasped, grabbed the ankle with both hands.

Tu's strength was such that the boot did not budge from the downed tough's throat. Tu stared down and addressed the man dispassionately.

"I could break your neck with no effort on my part whatsoever. Do you wish me to prove it?"

The young man's breathing grew ragged, raspy, as his air was cut off. He struggled weakly, ineffectually, at the boot pinning him. His eyes bulged with panic. "Don't . . . kill . . . me!" he managed.

"Where is Captain Quang?"

"I don't know. Only Vo knew."

Tu increased the pressure of the boot heel slightly. "The truth," he commanded sharply.

"That is the truth, I swear to you! Captain Quang contacted Vo . . . about killing the . . . American. Vo . . . would tell us . . . nothing. . . ."

"It is lucky for you," said Tu, "that I believe what you say." He stepped back. He glanced at the other hoodlums, who were starting to regain consciousness. He said to the man on the floor, "Take your friends and be gone. If any of your gang come back here, I will hunt you all down and kill you. You will leave my friend Quot alone, or you will die. Do you understand?"

The hoodlum pulled himself to his feet, massaging his throat. "I . . . understand. . . ." He was still out of breath, still frightened.

Tu stood and watched with his arms folded across his chest and a stern expression on his face as the hoodlum rousted his companions to their feet.

They fled, wobbly but throwing frightened backward glances over their shoulders. Then they were gone.

Tu relaxed. He turned to Quot. "There, that is done. I do not think they will be back to bother you."

"Nor do I, and I don't know how to repay you." Quot's

face split into one of his wide grins. "Except to offer you another beer on the house."

"Another time," said Tu. He started toward the door. "I must get back to Lai Khe with the news for Lieutenant Gaines that Captain Quang is alive. Contact me, Nguyen, if you should hear anything about Quang's whereabouts."

"I will," the man behind the bar promised. "And tell Lieutenant Gaines to be very careful until he is certain that Quang is dead."

"You don't know Scott Gaines" were Tu's final words to Quot on his way out the door. "It is Captain Quang who had better find a place to hide before the Tunnel Rats find him."

THIRTEEN

The hooch shared by Gaines's Tunnel Rats team was one of a staggered line of ramshackle wooden buildings interspersed with metal Quonset huts, mobile home trailers that functioned as offices, and the sandbagged bunkers that constituted the central area of the base.

They were lazing about during the heat of the day, bare-chested, waiting for Tu's return from Saigon or for any intelligence Captain Carter might come up with that would send them back to work.

Talk had finally found its way around again to what would happen when this war was over.

Some men needed to stay drunk or doped up when they went off duty, to keep the memories of home from becoming mental torture, but it was Gaines's opinion that talk of home—the World, as the grunt in 'Nam called it—was good for morale. If a soldier remembered what was waiting for him back in the World, he'd be more inclined to stay on top of staying alive.

DeLuca sat cross-legged on the wooden floor of their living quarters, paging through an issue of *Stars and Stripes*, reading an article Gaines had read earlier about the antiwar protest movement in the States.

"I'd always figured on going back to being a civilian after this mess was cleaned up. Now I'm not so sure I'd recognize the old U.S. of A."

Hidalgo snorted. "Are you saying you wouldn't go home? That's crazy talk, my man, or maybe you just didn't have it as good back in the World as yours truly." He stretched back on his bunk with his hands folded beneath his head. He stared with a contented sigh up at the ceiling. "Man, there are all kinds of foxy little senoritas back home pining away for the Hidalgo thing."

DeLuca chuckled. "Jody boy might have cleaned out the henhouse by the time you get home, stud."

Hidalgo shrugged from his reclining position. "So I have to start all over again meeting a new batch of ladies. There are worse things to look forward to, my man, believe it."

DeLuca flicked the newspaper forward, looking for the funnies. "Maybe you're right at that, Johnny. Them antiwar gals are into what they're calling free love. That's my kind of a price. Thanks, Johnny. Sometimes I lose track of the important stuff."

"Think nothing of it." Hidalgo propped himself up on an elbow and looked from his bunk across at Gaines. "What about you, Lieutenant? Ever think about when this war's over?"

There was not much regard for formal rank in a tightly knit unit like the Tunnel Rats. These men had plenty of respect for each other as men and as soldiers, but they had been through too much, had taken too much enemy fire together, for them to ever think of each other as anything other than buddies.

"I think about it," Gaines admitted. He sat in the open doorway of the hooch, leaning his back against the doorframe, gazing out across the midday activity of the base around them. He realized when Hidalgo spoke to him that he had been only barely following the idle banter of his teammates.

"He's thinking about Ann," said DeLuca. His tone was one of genuine concern. "Must be tough, guy," he said to Gaines, "taking fire with the lady in the restaurant and not even seeing her today."

"That lady's one tough tamale," said Hidalgo. "You got yourself one of the good ones there, Lieutenant."

Gaines was not surprised that these two could read his mind. Combat forges bonds between men, strong bonds. "You've got that right, Johnny," he said. "Yeah, I imagine Ann Bradley is handling herself just fine."

"I don't care how tough a lady is," said DeLuca, "it's only natural for a man to be concerned about his woman. Trust me on this, Lieutenant, I'm Italian. They need looking after whether they'll admit it or not, especially in a war zone. But that's a pacified area, that village she and Stevens visit, Hoa Phu."

"I'm also getting the itch to do something if we find out for sure that Quang is alive," Gaines said. "I'd like to know what Tu found out in Saigon."

"Here comes the captain," said Hidalgo.

They stepped outside to meet Carter, who approached with a grim visage and a determined stride from the direction of his bunker. When he reached them, Gaines felt a peculiar apprehension send chills up and down his spine.

"What is it, Captain?"

"We just got word," said Carter. "A supply column from

here was wiped out on its way to a fire base. It happened over in Hoa Phu."

"Ann—" The name shot out before Gaines could check it. He bit his tongue, steeling himself, readying himself for anything.

"There was a massacre," said Carter. "It looks like everyone in the village got it. These are just first reports out. Looks like it happened within the last thirty minutes, no more."

"Damn, damn, *damn*," said Hidalgo, looking down at the red clay at their feet.

"I don't care how you do it, but I want in on this," said Gaines to Carter.

"Figured you'd tear a chunk of it for yourself even if I couldn't wedge you into it," Carter told him. "You are in on it, the three of you. There were enough tunnels found in that area before it was pacified for me to authorize you to poke around. Get your armor and ammo and git. I've got a chopper warming itself up for you as we speak."

"Well, all right." DeLuca grunted. "You're right, sir, about us buying into this one even if you hadn't assigned us. This one is personal."

"There's still hope for Ann, Lieutenant," Hidalgo told Gaines. "Maybe she and Stevens hadn't reached that village when the massacre started."

Gaines's expression was like chiseled granite. "Let's find out," he said.

By the middle of the afternoon, Vien and his crew of young men and women were resting up for tonight's action, when they would pour through the tunnel and launch an assault against the U.S. Army installation at Lai Khe.

Some of the group slept against the wall of the dingy old

storehouse at the edge of the abandoned rubber plantation. A few others were reading political pamphlets.

Captain Quang waited. When no eyes were on him, he discreetly slipped through an open doorway. His absence would be short enough to suggest no more than a man stepping out to answer a call of nature.

The murky, gray-cloud sky and the gathering thunderheads did nothing to relieve the heat. The air outside the storehouse was without a breeze, almost too thick to breathe. *And then you will be avenged, my son,* Quang told the memory of Tsing that lingered in his heart, causing an empty ache in his soul.

He moved diagonally away from the storehouse. He looked up at the threatening sky once more before stepping into the treeline of the jungle, where the knee-high elephant grass ended.

He hoped for rain this night. Rain would keep people inside on the U.S. Army base, and security would be more lax. Their response would be slowed.

And Scott Gaines will die, Quang told his son's memory, *and you shall be avenged, no matter what it takes. I have nothing to live for now. I will die myself if that is what it takes to kill the American. . . .*

Quang had upscaled the objective of tonight's sneak attack. But he had not yet told Vien about the change in plans. He would do that in the moments before the assault was launched, when the committed young people of Vien's group were already highly keyed up. They would obey Quang's new orders willingly at that point even if it meant their own deaths.

Xong stood waiting at the prearranged rendezvous spot no more than a few paces inside the treeline but wholly concealed from view of those in the storehouse.

Quang nodded a greeting. "Lieutenant, I wish to commend you on the fine job you did in disposing of the traitor, Pham, who cost me my command."

"I only wish we had been more successful with the attempted elimination of Scott Gaines," said Xong.

"That matter will be seen to."

"Tonight? Are plans for the attack still on?"

"Precisely as they were when last we spoke. What of the investigation you mentioned at that time? Are the Americans any closer to learning that you are our eyes and ears in their midst?"

Xong smirked. "With Major Dow having assigned me to the investigation, how could there be any progress in the investigation?"

"What news of Gaines?"

"None, I regret to report, Captain. That Tunnel Rats team is off duty today. I have been able to learn nothing about them. Major Dow and I were at a meeting with them this morning, but nothing was said in my presence that we did not already know. But there is other news."

"And what is that? Do you speak of the massacre at Hoa Phu?"

Xong blinked his surprise. "But . . . the Americans have sealed off that area," he said. "They think no word has yet gotten out to the people."

"The people do not know yet," said Quang. "*I* know, Lieutenant, because I am not the people. I am Captain Quang, commander of the Seventh Battalion of the People's Army. I have ordered the remaining survivors of my command to go to the vicinity of the massacre and learn what they can."

"Is not the Vietcong responsible? The American convoy was looted—"

"We were not responsible. If another commander had

ordered the action, I would have known. No, it was bandits, Lieutenant Xong."

"You know they have taken a woman, then, an American nurse."

Quang nodded. "They were seen leaving the area. It was the brigand, Noh, who has complicated matters before. This time he will be dealt with. If my faith in my people is justified, I will soon know where they have taken the woman."

"You want the woman?"

"Of course."

"For ransom from the Americans?"

Quang made no attempt to hide his lack of patience with Xong. The man was valuable but hardly intelligent. "It would be most beneficial for me to interrogate this woman before tonight's action," he explained to Xong. "You are privy to much information about the Americans through your work with them, but to them you are an outsider. There are things the woman will know regarding the strength and placement of their personnel on the base, things which you may not be privy to. Such information could mean a great deal. I want our attack tonight through that tunnel to have the fullest impact on the Americans."

"I understand," said Xong. "I will make certain that you promptly receive any information regarding the matter that I may learn before tonight."

Quang heard Vien calling him from the direction of the storehouse. He stepped to the trunk of a balsa tree but remained concealed. Xong stood next to him. They saw Vien, and beside him was a narrow-framed, stoop-shouldered, wrinkle-faced peasant woman.

"That is Mrs. Truong," said Quang. "She is one of my people. She would only have come here if she had some information about where Khong Noh is holding the American woman."

"What about me?"

"Return to Lai Khe. Report if you learn anything, otherwise confine yourself to your regular duties."

Xong mulled this over. He did not like being left out, but he said, "As you say, Captain."

Quang waited until Xong turned and stepped away in the direction of a road a quarter-kilometer away. When he was gone from sight, Quang walked back through the elephant grass to join Vien and the woman.

"Mrs. Truong has important news," Vien greeted him. "She knows where the bandits have taken the American nurse."

"Very good," said Quang. "Order your people to prepare to march with me to Noh's camp. I want to question that woman. Khong Noh will not be gentle with her, and the Americans will be moving already to find her. We have no time to lose."

Vien nodded and darted off.

Quang turned to the woman. "Now, Mrs. Truong, you may tell me. Where have the bandits taken the American nurse?"

Consciousness was returning slowly to Ann Bradley. She was sitting. Her arms were behind her back, her wrists bound, her back braced by the narrow trunk of a young tree.

She opened her eyes. Pain coursed through her and made her groan, a fuzzy sound to her, slurred to her own ears.

A shifting image delineated itself into a young man in ragged peasant garb. He had been sitting across from her, observing her while she was unconscious. At the first sign of life from her, he leaped to his feet.

She watched him hurry away.

I'm alive! They did not kill me! The thought spurred her reviving awareness.

She looked around her. Nothing but a small patch of clearing in the jungle. Hot. Muggy. Insects. The screeching of monkeys and other animals.

She had a splitting headache that grew worse with each passing moment. She could feel the swollen bruise across one side of her head where she had been clipped with the butt of a rifle back at the village.

Images returned to her of what she had witnessed. The villagers. The soldiers. Phil. The little girl she had been tending before the ambush began. All of them dead.

The young man returned with the scar-faced, brutal-eyed man who had ordered the lad to strike her.

He stood before her, his hands on his hips. "I see you have decided to rejoin us, miss." His voice was guttural, very heavily accented.

"Who are you?" she asked, surprised at the steadiness of her own voice. She felt herself quivering inside.

"I am Khong Noh. You are my prisoner."

"I can see that, you ugly bastard. What's going on here?"

Noh's hands clenched into fists. "Watch your mouth, American bitch."

"You're not the Vietcong," she said. "Who are you?"

Noh calmed himself with visible effort. "You are quite right, dear lady. I am not charlie. Charlie would have killed you already."

"So what do you want?" Some of her anguish had entered her voice. Why did you have to kill all those people . . .?"

"I am holding you for ransom." Noh stepped forward. He squatted down before her. "And you had better hope they decide to buy you back."

She saw what he was about to do. She closed her eyes and bit her lip to keep from crying out as he roughly pawed and twisted her breasts cruelly.

Then Noh stood and stalked away, leaving the young man to squat across from her again, watching her.

She lowered her head and could not stem the tears that streamed across her cheeks. Burning tears of shame and helpless rage.

FOURTEEN

The Huey gunship banked around and descended into the pasture adjacent to Hoa Phu. Lazy livestock trudged out of the rotors' backwash, wholly unconcerned with the human drama so close by.

Gaines, DeLuca, and Hidalgo sat on the bench, gripping support straps, ready to hit the ground running. At the side door, a gunner sat behind his M-60, wary of any LZ.

Gaines and his men were outfitted in camo fatigues. They carried full combat gear—knife and chest webbing full of pouches with extra ammo and grenades, in addition to an M-16.

The scene from the chopper as they touched down was the kind of living nightmare that they would never forget.

Some of the huts had been burned to the ground. The column of American military vehicles that had been ambushed in the center of the village had been joined by all manner of U.S. and ARVN vehicles. Bodies were sprawled everywhere. Around the vehicles there was a concentration of fatigue-clad corpses draped in grotesque positions of violent death. The bodies of peasants were everywhere, their bodies pulped by weapon fire. Some of the females had been stripped and no doubt raped before being bayonetted or clubbed to death.

The view served only to fan the flames of furious anger pulsating through Gaines.

It was very possible that Carter's information had been incorrect; that his remarks on Ann's capture had been premature; that Gaines would find Ann's torn-apart corpse sprawled down there with the rest. But he wondered if a woman might not be better off dead than in the hands of human scum who could commit atrocities such as what he was now witnessing.

The three of them left the chopper.

The Huey lifted off.

They hoofed over to the cluster of U.S. military activity. Three-man teams were in the process of tagging and bagging the remains. Troopers were nosing around the remaining huts with great caution, searching for survivors. The loudest sound was the constant, industrious buzzing of flies.

A scene from hell, thought Gaines. A scene *of* hell, worse than anything in Dante's wildest imagination.

A man Gaines recognized turned from consulting with some of his junior officers and a pair of ARVN officers when he saw the Tunnel Rat team approaching.

Major Henry Otter was thick-bodied and had a red bull neck. He wore spit-polished boots, pressed fatigues, and reflecting sunglasses.

"What the hell are you doing here, Gaines?" he demanded with a thick Texas accent.

"Here to look around, Major."

"The hell you are, soldier. Under whose authorization?"

"Captain Carter's."

"What the hell does the frigging battalion S-2 have to do with my boys' getting cut to ribbons out here?"

Otter's verbal eruption was accompanied by bulging blood vessels in his neck and forehead and a deepening of the color in his face.

This one's close to the edge, thought Gaines. But he felt no malice toward Otter. These men—many of them no more than boys, really—had been under his command.

"Whoever did this had to go somewhere," Gaines said.

"I have choppers covering the entire area—"

"It's mighty thick jungle around here, Major," DeLuca opined. "S-2 thinks maybe whoever it was is better tracked on foot."

"You keep out of this, dog face, unless spoken to. And that's an order," Otter snapped. "And you," he continued to Gaines, "get on a radio and flag that Huey back here to airlift your asses. Where the hell was the Intel officer when we needed him, like when they told me this area had been pacified before I detailed these men to drive to their deaths."

"Cool down, Major," said Gaines.

Otter strutted forward and started to bring his fists up. "Don't you tell me to cool down, you mother-humping son of a bitch!"

Gaines stood his ground. "Maybe you're the one who should make radio contact with the base, Major. We're working for the same ends, to get the ones who killed your men and massacred this village."

"Goddamn mother-humping Vietcong."

"Maybe not," said Hidalgo. "The VC have been driven out of this area, Major. Could've been bandits."

Otter swiveled his glare on Hidalgo. "Maybe you'd like to share a cell in the brig with your buddy here." His glare took in DeLuca too. "I don't take kindly to enlisted men giving me crap."

"No one but you is giving anyone crap," said Gaines. "Leave these guys alone and pick on someone your own size, Major. I can take the heat. Are you going to get on that radio, or do you want me to call in for verification?"

A tableau held between these men for several taut seconds, during which Gaines expected the major to snap. The presence of this much death could get to anyone. Anyone.

Otter locked eyes with Gaines. Then he blinked. "You mother-humping sons stay right here until I get back."

He stalked off toward the comm jeep.

Otter would get his verification. Intelligence and Reconnaisance always got their way. Otter knew that.

The overripe sickly stench of death in the air made it extremely difficult for Gaines and his men to breathe. They did not have the scented gauze masks worn by most of the personnel working here.

Gaines stopped the first officer he encountered in charge of the bagging and tagging detail.

The first lieutenant pointed him to where the body of Phil Stevens still lay stretched out near the jeep.

There was no sign of Ann Bradley. There was no sign of any of the medicine or bandages Ann and Stevens had brought. The ambushers would hardly have left anything as valuable as that behind. The supply truck looked thoroughly ransacked too.

Gaines finished walking among the bodies and stood at the jeep that Phil and Ann had driven. The tag-and-bag detail had not managed to work its way over this far yet. The sheet covering Stevens was splotched with bloodstains.

Gaines braced himself against an emotional display that could dull the combat edge. But questions raced through his brain.

Where was Ann? What had they done with her?

Hidalgo and DeLuca stepped over from different directions after their inspection of the scene. Gaines followed their line of vision. He saw Major Otter strutting away from the communications jeep.

"Looks like the major forgot all about us," said DeLuca.

"Just like he was supposed to," said Hidalgo. "Now what?"

A vehicle full of journalists and new cameramen was being held back beyond the perimeter Otter had established around the hamlet. They were raising their voices to let everyone in the area know they didn't like the measure.

The network news media maintained an uneasy relationship with the military in-country. A lot of soldiers felt that the media was to blame for fanning the antiwar fervor back home.

"Let's nose around some," said Gaines.

The Tunnel Rats moved out to beyond the perimeter, where they began a slow walk around the village. They walked three abreast, at combat intervals, their eyes on the jungle beyond the communal pasture and fields around the village.

Gaines heard a faint voice.

Deluca heard it too. "What the hell's that?" he said.

Hidalgo said, "Sounds like a kid."

Gaines could make out the words then, but he could not yet tell from which direction they came.

"Lieutenant Scott, Lieutenant Scott," a small voice was calling from somewhere close by.

"Over there." Gaines nodded to his men.

Hidalgo and DeLuca swung their eyes and their M-16s in the direction of an underground shelter.

"What the hell?" Hidalgo grunted.

"I'll check it," said Gaines. "Cover me."

"Don't worry about that," said DeLuca. "Just be real careful, Lieutenant."

Hidalgo and DeLuca fell away to either side of the shelter. Gaines used a boot toe to nudge the camouflaged boards up and away. He stepped back quickly, then realized that his hunch had been correct. He lowered his rifle.

There was no danger here.

A pair of young, grimy faces stared up at him out of the shallow hole. A little boy and girl. The boy was seven or eight, the girl a few years younger. The boy had his arm around the girl. They were both trembling, the girl sobbing very quietly. The boy wore a New York Yankees cap.

"Lieutenant Scott..." the boy said in a small voice. "Bad men... gone?"

Gaines crouched down and extended a hand. "They're gone, Duong. You and your sister can come out now."

Gaines had accompanied Ann on one of her Saturday visits to Hoa Phu the month before, a day when Phil Steven's hangover had been worse than usual. He had spent his time with the boys and girls of the village, doing his best to teach them a sandlot version of baseball using a couple of sticks and a tennis ball. Duong and Gaines had taken a real liking to each other, and Gaines had left Duong the Yankees cap.

There was something heartbreaking about the pluckiness exhibited by Duong. Had he and his little sister been put here by their parents just as the massacre began? Most likely their parents were among the dead.

Duong let his sister be lifted from the hole, then he took the hand Gaines extended and came out too. Gaines squatted down to their level. He took the little girl's hand in his big paw and held it. That seemed to calm her down some. He looked at the little boy.

"I remember you, Duong. Tell your sister that you're safe now. We aren't going to hurt you."

"Yes, Lieutenant Scott."

As the boy translated for his sister, Gaines glanced at Hidalgo. "Johnny, go find someone to take care of these kids."

"Right, Lieutenant." Hidalgo bolted off.

The little faces of Duong and his sister were just starting to gaze around at the signs of devastation everywhere.

"Duong, I need your help," said Gaines.

"Yes, Lieutenant Scott. . . . You kill men who do this?"

DeLuca chuckled without humor. "Spunky little bugger."

"Yes, Duong," said Gaines, "I am going to kill who did this. Did you see it?"

"I only see bad men go away," said the boy. "They come past here." His eyes were looking around Gaines at the nearest hut. "They kill my mother and father?"

"I don't know, Duong. You must be very brave. Others will be here in a minute to take care of you and your sister. I have to go after the men who did this to your village. Do you understand?"

"Duong understand. The boy brought his full attention back to Gaines, his small face proudly serious. "You need . . . my help?"

"Very much. Tell me what you saw. The men who did this, could you tell if they were Vietcong?"

The boy shook his head. "Not charlie. I hear them laugh as they go past where we hide. They bandits, Lieutenant Scott. They say Americans think it will be charlie. I count eight men."

"Now we know better, Duong, thanks to you. But I need to know more. Did they take anyone with them?"

"They take American nurse lady," said the boy.

"Did you see which way they went, Duong?"

The boy nodded. "I see. I show you, Lieutenant Scott."

He held his sister's hand and led the way to a spot several yards down from where he and the little girl had remained concealed. He pointed.

The attackers had tried to cover their tracks with carefully arranged vines and leaves. Gaines saw machetes had hacked away at the greenery.

Hidalgo came over with a freckle-faced medic.

The young medic's open, sincere manner and the candy bars he handed out to Duong and his sister won him the kid's trust without hesitation.

But before the medic took them away, Duong asked Gaines, "You go after them now, Lieutenant Scott?"

"We're going after them, Duong. Thanks for your help, buddy. You're a good soldier."

The boy shook his head. "I am a good baseball player," he corrected.

The medic led the kids away.

Gaines watched them go. "God help us all," he said.

"If there is a God," Hidalgo grunted. "What the fuck do we do now, Lieutenant, go after them?"

DeLuca said, "What the fuck do you think, taco brains? We call in the troops"—he nodded back at Otter's men—"and those bandit motherhumpers will hear them coming a mile away and they'll sure enough waste the lady."

"This one's personal," said Gaines.

"Eight of them, three of us," mused DeLuca.

"We'll make the breaks," said Gaines. "Move out, Tunnel Rats."

Gaines and his men disappeared from sight into the wall of bright green that was the jungle. Gaines set the pace at a loping jog. Hidalgo and Deluca fell in behind him at combat intervals.

FIFTEEN

Tay, who in the wake of Ky's death had become Noh's new assistant, held Ann Bradley's dark hair bunched in his fist, cruelly lifting her face toward the Polaroid camera held by the bandit chief.

Noh clicked the shutter.

The flash of the bulb illuminated the interior of the military field tent and Ann Bradley's vacant stare.

Tay released her with a shove.

She fell back to lie upon the ground. Her ankles were bound. Her writs were tied behind her back.

She watched them without speaking.

Noh did not seem to mind. When the camera produced the picture, he tugged it free and studied it with a grunt of satisfaction.

"This will do, I think."

Tay looked at the picture. He nodded in agreement. "Should we kill her now?"

"Do not be impatient, Tay. A degree of subtlety is required in matters such as this."

"Sir?"

"I intend to demand a ransom of ten thousand dollars for this woman. They may want further proof that she is alive before paying the money."

"And when the money is paid?"

"What do you think?" Noh chuckled. "She can hardly be allowed to tell them everything she knows about us."

"You are a wise man, sir."

"A leader must be wise," Noh intoned, "or he cannot lead men. It is well that you understand this, Tay. Every man should understand his place. Had Ky understood this, I would not have felt obliged to kill him."

Noh enjoyed the fear that flashed in Tay's eyes when he said that.

Noh looked across at the woman. Though she did not understand their language, there was fear in her eyes too.

His eyes traveled along the contours of the woman's body: the curve of the hips, the way her breasts arched because her wrists were tied behind her. The only reason he had not taken her yet was that the longer he waited, the greater would be her fear and the more exciting the rape.

But soon, very soon . . .

The camp outside of this tent was quiet. Noh's men were spent from the fighting and the massacre of the village. Every man in the camp had raped more than one woman.

This evening he would send Tay into Saigon with an envelope addressed to the military commander at Lai Khe. The envelope would contain only the photograph.

Noh would let a day or so go by before telephoning the Americans with his ransom demand. He wondered what sort of a split, if any, he should allow the men of his band.

Perhaps, he thought, the thing to do would be to take the money and start over somewhere else. He could manipulate Tay into helping him kill the others—a couple of bursts of automatic fire from behind would take care of that—and then it would be easy enough to kill Tay. Then the ten thousand dollars would be his alone. In this part of the world, ten thousand dollars could make a man a king.

That, thought Noh, would be real power. . . .

His reverie was interrupted by stirrings from without, the muttering, surly voices of his men and a cooler, commanding voice that he did not recognize.

"Tay, see who it is."

Tay started to obey, but before he could step outside, the endflap of the tent was flung back and two men stepped in.

Noh could see a third figure standing outside the tent aiming an AK-47 at his men.

These were not Americans! They wore the black uniform of the Vietcong. One of them held an AK-47 aimed at Noh and Tay.

The man who held no rifle Noh recognized as Ngai Quang, a unit commander of the Vietcong. It was Quang's voice Noh had heard from outside the tent.

Quang locked eyes with Noh but spoke to the man holding the AK-47.

"Watch them carefully, Vien. Shoot them down if they try anything."

"As you say," said Vien.

Noh felt his throat go dry. But he was not wholly intimidated; his life had been one of constant conflict and violence.

"What are you doing here, Captain Quang?"

"You know me, then. Good, that will save time." Quang glanced down at Ann Bradley for the first time, not out of compassion, merely an acknowledgment of her presence. "I have come for the woman. I will take her with me."

Noh started to lunge forward, lifting his grasping fingers toward Quang's throat. "I will kill you if you—" Then rational thought returned as Vien swung the AK-47 in Noh's direction.

Noh stepped back. He lowered his arms. "I do not understand, Captain Quang. What does this woman matter to you?"

"That is no concern of yours. I want her. That is all that need concern you," said Quang. "If you wish to put up a struggle, you and your men will die."

"Captain Quang, this is hardly a proper show of gratitude. You are a powerful man in the Vietcong. You should be grateful for what my men and I did today in that village."

"I do not object to the death of those Americans," said Quang, "nor to the decimation of a village that was friendly to the Americans."

"Then why—"

"I want the woman," said Quang. "I am taking her." He unsheathed an American combat knife worn on his belt. He leaned forward, intending to slice away the twine binding her wrists and ankles.

Noh rapidly calculated his options. He did not want to lose the money this woman represented to him. He must risk everything.

"Stop," he barked.

Quang looked at Noh with genuine curiosity. "What did you say?"

"You are not a man," said Noh. "You are a coward, Captain Quang." He nodded at Vien. "You let others do your killing. You are afraid to fight me for the woman."

"I am afraid of no man."

Noh gestured at the knife Quang held. "You like knives? Good. So do I." He reached behind his back and produced a knife similar to Quang's. "Do you dare to fight me to the death for the woman, Captain, or am I right in calling you a coward?"

Vien watched his commander for instructions. Quang caught Vien's eye and nodded once. Vien left the tent.

Noh dismissed Tay and faced Quang over the bound woman.

"I understand your son died yesterday," Noh taunted, making small circular motions with his knife. "I will kill you now, Captain, and there will be one less family of worthless cowards in our country."

"Dog!" Quang's temper erupted. "You dare to insult the memory of my heroic son and the family whose loss I mourn? You will *die!*"

He lunged, striking with his knife blade at the region of Noh's heart.

Noh deflected the thrust with a straightened left arm. His left fist snaked up to clamp around Quang's arm. At the same time he slashed at Quang's throat.

They struggled like that for nearly half a minute, locked together in a match of strength and will. The only sound in the tent for that half minute was their labored breathing.

Then Noh kicked out with a booted foot.

The unexpectedness of the movement caught Quang off guard. He tripped and went down, but he took Noh with him and they remained locked in a murderous embrace, each one trying to hold back the other's searching knife blade.

They landed first with Noh on the bottom, Quang on top, their grimacing, sweating faces practically touching.

"You are a brute savage," Quang hissed. "You are evil. I am a trained fighter and I fight for my people, my family. Give up, Noh. You are finished."

"Never!" Noh roared. With a renewed surge of strength, he flung himself to the side, toppling Quang, and reversing their position.

The struggle continued, two knife points pressing and pulling back, each man knowing that this could not last much longer.

One of them would die.

Ann Bradley watched with vacant eyes, unable to rise from her prone position.

Since he was point man, Gaines was the first one to hear the murmur of voices somewhere ahead of them.

The jungle held them in its smothering, humid embrace, a world of almost blinding green overhead where palm fronds and vines blocked direct sunlight, and the chirping, screeching cacophony of unseen animal life that grated constantly on the senses. Except for the traces of the bandits having hacked their way through the thick jungle, there was no trace of humanity.

They started forward very slowly on upward-sloping terrain, three abreast but spread out, advancing without a sound.

They paused as one when they came upon a clearing around the crumbling remains of what had once been a religious shrine. They crouched low.

Gaines counted five men in the process of hurriedly breaking camp, conversing among themselves as if in disagreement.

The lack of uniforms and the heavy firepower testified that these were the bandits. Each man toted an AK-47 assault rifle.

There was no sign of life around the field tent—and no sign of Ann Bradley.

Where was the bandit leader? Were he and Ann together? The questions raced through Gaines's mind. If they were in the tent, why hadn't they come out?

Five bandits.

The kid at the village had counted eight men. . . .

A warning chill raced up and down Gaines's spine.

He twisted around just as a figure materialized amid the vines and foliage and tree trunks behind them.

The features of the figure could not be determined, but Gaines had no trouble identifying the shape tracking on them as the barrel of an assault rifle.

"Behind us!" Gaines said. *"Down!"*

Hidalgo and DeLuca did not take time to question or see for themselves. They flung themselves down without hesitation.

The assault rifle being aimed at them hammered out an extended, sweeping burst.

Bullets shredded jungle greenery less than twelve inches above their heads. Some of the bullets overshot into the ranks of the bandits.

Gaines squeezed off one shot from his M-16.

After a violent burst of exploding red, the target pitched backward to the ground out of sight.

DeLuca chuckled. "Head shot. Way to go, Lieutenant."

They twisted around, staying low, as a couple of bandits pulled off crazed and aimless rounds.

Two other bandits were in the process of hurling themselves for cover behind the dilapidated shrine.

Gaines, Hidalgo, and DeLuca opened fire together. The pair of bandits firing on them toppled.

Gaines then triggered a burst at those seeking cover behind the deserted shrine, but he was a shade too late. The bandits returned a blistering fire that momentarily had Gaines and his men hugging the mucky jungle floor.

"Try to keep them there," said Gaines. "I'll move around to their side."

"Aw, you get to have all the fun, Lieutenant," Hidalgo muttered.

There came a break in the incoming fire.

Hidalgo and DeLuca lifted themselves to open fire on those pinned down.

Gaines fell away, pushing through the jungle. He kept under cover as he moved toward a point that he figured would afford him a line of fire on those behind the shrine.

Then they saw him. They opened fire on him. They missed. Gaines raked both men with enough fire to blow their bodies apart, splashing their insides across the vine-covered shrine. *Damn!* He had wanted them to surrender. He'd wanted them alive!

Quiet descended upon the clearing. For an entire minute, Gaines held his position while Hidalgo and DeLuca held theirs. No one spoke, for to do so could draw fire from someone lying in wait nearby.

Two bandits remained unaccounted for.

Gaines could wait no longer. "I'm going in to take a look," he called.

"Got you covered, Lieutenant," DeLuca responded. "Watch your ass."

Gaines broke from cover and was halfway to the structure when a young man bolted from where he had been hiding throughout the firefight.

Tay could think only of escape.

Everything had happened so suddenly. First the appearance of Captain Quang and his men, and then this attack!

Tay had slain many men and women and children this day, but he had no stomach for a fight now. *The Americans will not shoot me in the back!* The thought pushed him onward across the clearing, away from the shrine as fast as he could run. I *will* get away!

Gaines aimed from the hip and squeezed off a round that blew away the running punk's kneecap.

The bandit reeled around like an ice skater losing his balance, went down, and immediately began screaming.

Gaines strode over. The kid was squealing, writhing about on his back, both hands blindly gripping the shin beneath the kneecap that was a mess of shattered bone, gristle, and welling blood.

Gaines aimed his M-16 down, but the bandit was wholly oblivious to this, so blinded was he by shock and pain. Gaines had to get his attention first.

He pulled back his right boot and kicked the kid in the side of the head. The kid kept screaming as if he had not noticed, so Gaines kicked him again, a blow not to cave in the skull or render the bandit unconscious but hard enough to get a response.

The kid stopped screaming. He whipped his glazed eyes in Gaines's direction, staring up the length of the M-16 aimed between his eyes. His mouth was a quivering hole from which whimpers and saliva sputtered.

"Where is the woman?" Gaines demanded in the local dialect. "Tell me, damn you."

"C-Captain . . . Quang . . ." the bandit whimpered weakly.

As he said it, his eyes shifted for a pain-wracked moment at the field tent nearby. Then another wave of agony washed through him and he went back to screaming.

Scenes of the massacre at Hoa Phu flashed before Gaines's eyes.

"See you in hell, shitface."

He triggered a round from the M-16 that disintegrated

the bandit's head in a messy splash across the ground. Then he turned and started toward the field tent. He restrained himself from running.

He realized that he was more keyed up than he wanted to be. The massacre, Ann in enemy hands . . . He told himself he would be doing Ann no good if he were to get his own head blown off.

Hidalgo and DeLuca emerged from where they had been covering him. Gaines motioned his instructions. They nodded.

DeLuca stood his ground, watching for danger.

Hidalgo approached the field tent from one side, Gaines from the other.

When they stood at either end of the tent, Gaines held up three fingers.

Hidalgo nodded his understanding.

Gaines nodded once, twice, three times.

On the third nod, he and Hidalgo each pulled back an endflap, stepping back as they did so to avoid possible fire from inside. They looked inside.

They lowered their rifles when they saw the corpse.

The dead man had been big for a Vietnamese. He lay on his back. A combat knife was buried to the handle in his heart.

Gaines stepped inside. Hidalgo remained where he was.

"Who the hell is that?" DeLuca called.

"Name's Khong Noh," said Gaines. "He was in a dossier the ARVN passed along on major criminals in the province."

"So where's Ann?" asked Hidalgo.

Gaines bent down and picked up three lengths of rope that lay tangled together across the tent from the body. He stepped outside.

"Noh had her. From what that punk said before I

greased him, Quang came by and snatched her away. I'd say Quang and Noh fought over Ann. With Noh dead, his boys didn't have any more stomach for killing. They let Quang take her away without a fight and were fixing to cut out themselves when we showed up."

"So Quang is alive like you thought," Hidalgo said. "Then Ann's alive too."

"But where the hell did they go?" said Hidalgo, studying the smothering, towering walls of green that closed in from every side. "I don't see a trace."

"We won't find a trace," said Gaines, although he, too, was closely scrutinizing the surrounding jungle. "Quang bested Noh because he's a better man. He knows this jungle well enough not to leave a trail."

"So they're out there somewhere," said Hidalgo, his eyes following those of Gaines and DeLuca, "and we don't have any frigging idea where. God fucking *damn* it."

"With the way Quang feels about you, Lieutenant," said DeLuca, "we'd better find them fast. It won't go good for her if he finds out she's your sweetheart."

Gaines took one last look at the tent and the remains of the shrine and the bodies scattered about.

"This is a dead end," he said in disgust. "There's nothing we can do here. Let's get back to the base."

SIXTEEN

The loft was sweltering.

Captain Quang angrily lashed out with the back of his hand.

Ann Bradley saw the blow coming, but she did not attempt to dodge or block it. She took the backhand slap full across the side of her face, the blow striking with such force that she pitched sideways from the empty packing crate of rotting wood upon which she'd sat while Quang interrogated her and the one called Vien looked on.

"You will tell me what I want to know, Nurse Bradley." He stood over her, his voice full of loathing and contempt. "Or you will die."

It was the first time he had used her name. He had glanced at her dog tags, then thrown them aside. He had showed her the map. She had refused to look at it, and so he struck her.

The fires of madness burned in his eyes.

She looked past him at Vien.

The younger man's expression shone with the intense commitment of a true zealot. Maybe that was madness too, she thought, but the VC commander was the one she had most to fear.

In her estimation, Captain Quang had edged into total insanity.

"You will kill me anyway, Captain Quang."

"Ah, you know me."

She nodded. "Yes, and I know what happened to your command. I know about the loss of your son."

He flinched as if he had been physically slapped. "Then you will perhaps better understand your own situation when I tell you what I know about you, Nurse Bradley. You see, I recognize the name from the newspaper accounts of a shooting last evening at a restaurant in Saigon. I know that you are Scott Gaines's lover."

"We are not lovers. We were friends out for a dinner date." She tried to ignore the throbbing ache where he'd slapped her. "And what does Scott Gaines have to do with anything?"

"He has everything to do with why you are here, dear lady. Do not try subterfuge with me. You know as well as I that your Lieutenant Gaines's team of Tunnel Rats were responsible for the destruction of my command and the death of my son."

"Lieutenant Gaines was following orders from someone else," she said, "even if what you say is true. In any event, I know nothing about it."

"Your lies will buy you nothing but pain, Nurse Bradley. There are ways to make you talk. A woman is particularly vulnerable to such forms of persuasion. I would advise you to cooperate with us."

She happened to notice Vien as Quang quietly spoke this threat. The younger man winced at the reference to torture, and a queasy, uncertain look touched the determined set of his boyish face. He stared straight ahead, avoiding her eyes.

"I will not help you," she told Quang.

"You will help us," he countered, "whether you believe that now or not." He stood before her. "This is your last chance to avoid suffering, dear lady. Now, tell me where I can find the man Gaines."

He thrust the piece of paper at her face.

This time she looked at it. It was a detailed diagram of the base at Lai Khe.

She had recognized Quang the moment she saw him. As regional Vietcong commander, his photograph had been circulated to all U.S. and ARVN personnel at Lai Khe.

She had known from the start that there was no reason to rejoice when Quang showed up at the bandit camp to fight their leader to death for her.

They had traveled hard and fast on foot through rugged terrain. The men to either side of her never released their hold. Even when a vine caught her ankle and she tripped, they continued on without stopping, dragging her roughly several paces before she regained her balance.

She awoke fully during the trek through the jungle. But with that blessing came an intensifying of aches and pains throughout her body.

She did not give them the satisfaction of making a sound of protest or pain. She told herself she would take whatever they could dish out.

They had brought her to this warehouse on this vacated rubber plantation, to this loft where there did not seem to be enough air to breathe and the heat was overwhelming.

There was a small group of them waiting at the warehouse, young men and a few women about Vien's age. The group was armed. They were curious but were shunted off to the far end of the warehouse, well beyond earshot, by the young man who had accompanied Quang and Vien to the bandit camp.

Vien had climbed up to the loft. Quang motioned her to climb the ladder, which she did. Quang followed, and the "interrogation" had begun.

She looked away from the map of the base. "I will tell you nothing."

His rage again erupted.

This time she did not see it coming, and the blow pitched her to the floor. He slapped her where she had been struck with the rifle butt. She fought off the cloud of nausea and unconsciousness that threatened to overwhelm her. The throbbing, pulsating pain only grew worse, but she held on to a bleary-eyed sort of consciousness.

She did not move from where she landed across the grimy floorboards of the loft.

Quang stepped closer. He nudged her shoulder none too gently with the toe of a boot and rolled her over. She kept her eyes closed, her mouth slack, her breathing deep. He released her, allowing her body to roll back facedown.

Quang stood, and he and Vien launched into a low-key but emphatic disagreement of some kind. She did not understand the language, but they could only have been disagreeing about her.

Vien had put off confronting his commander for as long as he could, but he had known since they'd climbed up to the loft with the woman that he could not blindly accept Quang's authority in this matter.

Quang spoke first.

"Awaken her. Torture her. I want her to tell us where Gaines is likely to be tonight when we attack."

Vien cleared his throat and straightened his back. "I regret, sir, that I cannot follow your orders."

Quang turned slowly to look at him with an imperious, penetrating stare. "Do I hear you correctly, Vien? You will awaken this woman. I want that information from her."

"I will not be a party to torture."

"You knew when we went to Noh's encampment that we would interrogate her."

"You said nothing of torture. She is a woman."

"As are some of our ablest combatants," Quang snapped. "Why should that matter?"

"She is an American woman. I thought she would be easily intimidated and made to talk. I did not think it would come to this."

Quang smiled enigmatically. "And so the noble ideals of the revolutionary are tested by the cold demands of reality, and the revolutionary fails the test because he is only a boy playing games who has no place in the real world of sacrifice and struggle."

"My group and I are prepared to make the ultimate sacrifice tonight when we attack through the tunnel," Vien countered. "We will give our lives to fight to drive out the imperialist invaders if called to do so. That is the depth of our commitment, Captain Quang. Do not question it."

"I did not think I would have a discipline problem with you, Vien."

"I am sorry, Captain, but I question your motives behind this interrogation."

"You dare to disobey me—"

"This woman is a nurse, Captain. She is not a combatant. We cannot torture her. I do not mean to be disrespectful, but I cannot allow myself to become a torturer of women."

Quang seethed wordlessly for thirty seconds.

Vien had no doubt as to what Quang was thinking.

Quang would weigh this "discipline problem" against

the larger problem of risking trouble with those he was counting on to execute the attack tonight on the American base.

Quang blinked. Emotion vanished from his face. His expression became enigmatic again.

"Very well, Vien. Perhaps you are right. We will question her later. Let us rest up for now."

Without another word, Quang went to the ladder and climbed down from the loft, leaving Vien alone with the unconscious woman.

Vien sighed his relief. He was glad the confrontation had not escalated. He wondered what he should do about the doubts vexing him. He wondered if he and his friends were not being used by Quang as pawns in a personal blood fued between the commander and the American, Scott Gaines.

Quang had told Vien he wanted to question the woman about the placement of Americans on the base. This had sounded most reasonable to Vien.

But when it came time to actually interrogate the woman, Quang had seemed concerned only with the matter of where he could find the man he considered responsible for the death of his son.

Vien knew the background of this mission. He had originally expected to go into battle tonight with Quang's son. At first he had been relieved to learn that Tsing's father intended to carry out the strike, for in truth the strike would be a highly effective terrorist action if properly executed.

Vien had nothing but hatred in his heart for the Americans. But he cared about his friends who had come with him on this mission. He intended to keep a close watch on Captain Quang if it seemed that his fixation with this Gaines would in any way endanger lives.

Vien went to the ladder. With a final look at the

woman, he climbed down, disappearing from her line of vision. She watched through barely lifted eyelids.

Vien had interceded on her behalf, she knew not why. He was of a different stripe than Quang, of course. Quang was a military pragmatist. He probably thought of his dementia as the amorality of war, that worthy ends justified any means necessary, including torture and the murder of innocent civilians.

She knew of plenty of American commanders with the same point of view.

She knew only two things with absolute certainty at this moment.

First, Quang intended to attack the base at Lai Khe.

And second, she had to get the hell out of here.

There was a single square window set in the wall several feet across the loft from where she lay.

Quang would surely place a guard at the foot of the stairs. The possibility existed that the guard would be instructed to look in on her, to call Quang when she came to so he could resume his interrogation.

She had to get away from here. She had to get back to the base, to warn them of the impending attack.

The fact that Quang had massed this force here at this deserted plantation warehouse indicated that the attack would come tonight. Quang had commanded one of the underground tunnel battalions of the VC. They would attack tonight, and it would be a tunnel operation. The map of the base, Quang's involvement, the armed group assembled here, waiting . . . it could add up no other way.

Scott Gaines was a marked man. No matter what Quang did this night, he would slay Scott or he would die trying, she was certain.

She inched her way to the edge of the loft and peeked over at the open area below.

The rest of the group had been allowed back into the warehouse. They lounged about here and there, some of them sleeping in the late-afternoon heat. She did not see Quang or Vien.

Sure enough, there was a sentry posted at the bottom of the stairs leading up to the loft. Apparently, he had not been instructed to check on her.

Trying not to make a sound, she moved back across the loft to the window.

She cursed to herself when she saw what the shadows had obscured until her close-up inspection of the window.

A hasp had been screwed into the window frame and was padlocked. There was no way of opening the window.

She rested back against the wall next to the window and sank to the floor. She could not hold back a sigh of defeat and frustration she felt to the core of her being.

She *had* to escape! But there was no way she could.

No way in hell.

SEVENTEEN

Dusk would fall early tonight.

The ceiling of hovering thunderheads was taking on an ominous gunmetal-gray hue. The rumblings of thunder were now almost constant. The humidity was oppressive, but it had not yet started to rain.

A chopper had been waiting for Gaines and his team when they got back to Hoa Phu from the site of the firefight with Khong Noh's bandits.

The Tunnel Rats hustled directly to Captain Carter's bunker upon touchdown back at the base.

An urgent restlessness was building to a fevered pitch in Gaines's gut. It had been bad enough worrying about Ann out there in the bush, but now, stalled as they were, he had difficulty reining in his frustration.

Carter was waiting for them with a concerned expression that said he shared Gaines's feelings. He was waiting alone, and that told Gaines something else.

Gaines could not keep the disappointment or the frustration out of his voice as he asked, "Tu isn't back from Saigon yet?"

Carter shook his head. "Not a word."

"He'll be back before dark, Lieutenant," said Hidalgo, "just like you told him to."

"And don't worry, Lieutenant." DeLuca nodded in agreement. "He'll have what you sent him for: some word on Quang. That Kit Carson of ours hasn't struck out yet."

"I am worried," said Gaines. "We all are. Until Tu gets back, we're dead-ended on the Quang angle. We know he's alive. We need to know where. Where does he have Ann?"

"Something is in the wind, all right," said Hidalgo, "and it ain't just the smell of rain."

"It don't add up any other way," said DeLuca. "Why the hell else would Quang show up at Noh's camp and fight the punk to the death over Ann? Quang wouldn't give a shit if Noh was holding a dozen Americans. He'd be glad to see Noh wipe out as many of their common enemy as he felt like."

"Quang wants information from her," said Gaines. "That's the only answer. You're right, guys, it doesn't add up any other way."

"So what else do we have?" asked Carter. "We can't be strung up by the thumbs on this."

"We're not," said Gaines. "I think this is tied in with the thievery that's been going on."

"The spy angle." Carter nodded. "Of course."

"If Quang has a spy planted on this base in the ARVN detachment," said Gaines, "then that spy can tell us how to find Quang. Then we'll know where Ann is."

"You said you thought those thefts were just the tip of an iceberg," DeLuca recalled.

"If Quang put a man in place, it would have to be a big shot for it to be worthwhile," said Hidalgo.

"The background check on Major Dow and his boy Xong hasn't come through yet," said Carter.

"I still don't like the smell of either one of those guys," growled Hidalgo.

"Ditto," said DeLuca.

"Captain, why don't you invite the major over for a little chat," Gaines suggested. Tell him to come alone, not to bring Xong with him."

"That can be arranged," said Carter.

He reached for his phone, and a moment later he had Dow himself on the line.

As per Carter's suggestion, the ARVN officer came alone. Gaines sensed a wary uneasiness on the part of Dow, although the Viet major maintained his ramrod-straight military bearing. As before, Dow had an automatic pistol holstered at his hip.

"Gentlemen"—he nodded stiffly—"you have my sincere sympathy for the loss of your comrades who were killed today at Hoa Phu. Rest assured that the Army of the Republic of Vietnam is taking every step to—"

"We're more interested," Carter interrupted, "in knowing what's turned up in your investigation of those thefts and break-ins we've been having."

"Yes," said Dow. "The spy business. Uh, may I ask, Captain, why it was you did not want me to bring Lieutenant Xong with me?"

"Stop beating around the bush, Major," said Hidalgo. "We want answers."

Dow looked puzzled. "Beating around the bush?" he repeated.

"He means you're not answering the question," said Gaines. "Tell us what you've learned and cut the bullshit."

Dow did not register anger. Instead, he sighed, a strange sound coming from him.

"I do not beat around the bush," he said. "You know, of course, that it was Lieutenant Xong whom I placed in charge of the investigation."

"That's why we don't want him along," said Carter. "Among other reasons."

"You said he was your best man," Gaines recalled.

"I was sadly mistaken, gentlemen. When Lieutenant Xong told me a short time ago that he had spent this entire day on the base investigating the possibility of a spy in our ranks and that he had learned nothing, I became skeptical. You see, gentlemen, I, too, believe there to be a spy among us here at Lai Khe. And I am afraid it is Lieutenant Xong."

"Why do you think that?" asked Gaines.

"I checked on the Lieutenant," said Dow. "He left the base twice. He lied to me. That may not be proof, granted, but I think he should be questioned."

"You didn't exactly break your neck getting over here to tell us about Xong," Carter pointed out.

"I came directly over upon receiving your call, Captain."

"That's what he means," said DeLuca. "We had to call you."

"If what I suspect is true," said Dow, "then I view Xong's betrayal and treachery as a personal affront."

"And there's the death of that VC prisoner, Pham, last night," Hidalgo pointed out. "If Xong is on charlie's payroll, Pham's death was no suicide."

"May I ask why you gentlemen think Lieutenant Xong is a spy?"

"Quang would have placed his man at the top," said Gaines. "You and Xong and a couple of others are the top."

"Then you suspect me, as well, of being a spy?" Dow did bristle this time.

Gaines got to his feet. "Let's track down Xong," he said. "We need to talk to him." He saw no reason to mention to Dow the developments after the massacre at Hoa Phu.

Dow watched the others climb to their feet. He was considering his options.

"Very well," he said. "I see that I must prove my honesty, my integrity, to you. I wish it were not so, I wish you trusted me as a soldier and a friend. But I will prove to you whose side I am on. I will personally assist in the apprehension and questioning of Lieutenant Xong."

The restless pressure continued to build inside Gaines.

"Stuff the pretty speech, Major. You'll help us and we'll question him."

"As you wish."

"Where is he?"

"Come, I will take you to him."

Gaines glanced to Carter.

Carter nodded his approval.

Gaines said to Dow, "So take us."

Gaines left the tent with Dow. Hidalgo and DeLuca came right behind them. They crossed the busy base in determined strides in the direction of the ARVN headquarters.

Along the way, Dow said, "We have learned from our intelligence sources among the civilian population that there is credence to the rumor that Captain Quang survived the attack on his tunnels yesterday."

"We've learned the same thing," said Gaines.

"And yet it was Xong who first brought the rumor to our attention," Dow continued. "Would he have done this if he were a spy?"

"Sure he would have," DeLuca said from behind them.

"They knew that would be common knowledge soon enough."

Hidalgo nodded. "Xong just told us that to throw suspicion off himself."

Dow nodded at the command bunker they were fast approaching. "We will find Lieutenant Xong inside there if he is where he should be this time."

"How do we play this, Lieutenant?" DeLuca asked.

"Light and easy," said Gaines. "Fall away about here, you two. Take a position to either side of the front of that bunker in case he raises a fuss and tries to bust out. Major, you and I are going in that bunker after him. Remember, everyone, there are questions we've got for the lieutenant. We want him alive."

Hidalgo and DeLuca were just starting to split off when Lieutenant Xong emerged from the ARVN command bunker.

Xong saw the approaching foursome, and he must have read something in what he saw. His demeanor reminded Gaines of a cornered rodent. Xong broke away from the front of the bunker and started into a dead-heat run in the opposite direction.

The group gave chase. Gaines and Dow, in the lead, unholstered their pistols.

Xong's charging run took him smack dab into a cul-de-sac formed by three bunkers near the one he'd bolted from. The instant he realized this, he spun around on his pursuers from about fifty feet away, and unholstered his pistol.

Gaines started to yell at him to stop, that they did not want to kill him. He was cut off by the sharp bark of Major's Dow's pistol.

Xong emitted a sharp grunt of pain. He spun around and fell, the pistol flying from his fingers. He landed in a face-down, twisted position and did not move.

Gaines had two immediate reactions: a sinking feeling in the pit of his stomach and an almost overwhelming urge to strangle Major Dow with his bare hands.

The moment held for several seconds.

The gunshot was bringing all manner of inquiring yells. Soldiers, Vietnamese and American, were approaching on a run from every direction.

Hidalgo and DeLuca lowered their rifles. They strode over for a look at the dead man.

"I told you we wanted him alive, Major," Gaines said.

"But he was about to point his weapon at us. I did not want to see one of us killed. . . ."

Hidalgo and DeLuca strode back over from having examined Xong.

"Deader than shit," said DeLuca.

"Right between the eyes," Hidalgo added with dry sarcasm. "Nice shooting, Major."

"Get out of here, Major," said Gaines in a barely controlled voice. "Just get out of here."

"I'm sorry," said Dow. "I did not realize—"

"Get out of my sight, Major."

This time the Vietnamese man caught the threat of violence coursing beneath the words. "Yes . . . I'm sorry. I only mean to help," he said weakly in a contrite voice. He turned abruptly and walked away.

Gaines watched him go. The anger in him was receding. He reminded himself that he could not afford that emotion, not with Ann's life at stake.

Ann.

They had just lost their last lead to Quang. . . .

It had not taken long for Gaines and his men to disengage from the shooting of Xong. The loose ends involved were being seen to by others. The ARVN MPs and their internal security were also involved. Gaines knew that, for the time being, he would have to leave any suspicions of Dow to them.

When they returned to the Intel bunker a short time later, Carter stood waiting outside for them.

Tu stood next to him.

The Kit Carson scout and the Tunnel Rats team nodded greetings to each other, then Gaines delivered a very brief report of the shooting to Carter.

Carter frowned. "I could request their MPs detain Dow and turn him over to us."

"Thought about it," said Gaines. "They would never consent to that without some proof, and we don't have a shred."

"We could always take the gook major for a ride," De-Luca suggested. "Under duress. If he's in Quang's back pocket, he might know where Quang is."

"If Dow is a plant, he's too high up to be caught making direct contact with Quang," said Gaines. "As an extra safety precaution, he probably doesn't even know where Quang is. He would have used Xong to make contact. Anyway, we still don't have any proof, and we could be wrong."

"Then listen up to what Tu found out in Saigon," said Carter. "Other things are happening."

"Ngai Quang is alive," Tu told them. "You know this after what happened at Hoa Phu, Captain Carter told me. But I tell you now that Captain Quang also sent the gunmen who tried to kill you in the restaurant last night."

"Clears that up at least." Gaines grunted. "Any leads on Quang's possible whereabouts?"

"Not directly," Carter put in, "but wait until you hear the rest."

"On way to catch bus back to base," said Tu, "I hap-

pened to see a woman who has been an informer in the
past. She has never told me anything great and she has her
own reasons. She is married to a student radical named
Vien. She informs because she wants those he serves put
away so he will stay home with her at night as a husband
should, do you understand?"

"Never stayed home much while I was a husband." De-
Luca chuckled.

"Which is probably why you're paying alimony and
child support," said Hidalgo.

"Skip it, guys," said Gaines. "What did this woman tell
you?" he asked Tu.

"Vien's wife was very unhappy. He told her that he
would not be home this night. That he may not come back,
that he may die tonight for his cause. He told her that he
has been chosen by Captain Quang to lead an attack on this
base. She did not want to tell the Americans. She does not
want her husband to die. I took time to explain to her that
many good men would die. That Vien and Quang must be
stopped and that I would try to help Vien so he does not
die. She told me these things, but she did not know where
they were."

"We've already stepped up security measures," said
Carter. "This confirms your hunch that something big is
brewing."

"If Quang is involved," said Gaines, "it has to mean a
tunnel operation."

"Damn right," said Carter. "I've already got the other
teams heading out to look for that tunnel, and you're heading out with them."

Thunder boomed overhead, and the first sprinkling of
raindrops began.

EIGHTEEN

The heat of the loft, the fatigue, the shock of everything that had happened and the overwhelming frustration when she realized she was hopelessly trapped, had conspired to put Ann Bradley in a fitful sleep.

She awoke to being roughly shaken. She opened her eyes. She was stretched across the floor boards of the loft, against the wall under the locked window.

She pressed her hands to the floor. It seemed to require a monumental effort merely to straighten those supporting arms, righting herself to a sitting position.

She thought she heard the hurried shuffle of feet across the floor of the loft, moving away from her. She could not be certain. Her faculties were returning, but not all at once. She worked to steady her whirling senses. She succeeded.

She was alone in the loft.

Someone had come up here, shaken her awake, and gone back down the ladder before she could fully come to.

She could hear voices inside the old warehouse, from

below the loft where she could not see, but she could not understand the words being spoken.

She glanced around at the window.

It was rapidly growing darker outside, the gloom of night spreading earlier than usual because of the overcast sky.

Something was different.

She saw it then.

And for a moment she didn't believe it.

The lock on the window had been removed!

She frowned to herself. Someone had come up here, unlocked the window, shook her awake, and fled down the ladder before she had been able to fully come to her senses.

Who? she wondered. And why?

The hell with whether or not it made any sense, she decided. She wanted *out!*

She lifted the window open. Then she paused to consider another possibility.

Could it be a trap? But to what purpose? she reasoned. If they wanted to kill her, why some elaborate ruse to make her think she was escaping? That really didn't make sense, she decided.

There was no time for further questioning. She had her chance, and she would take it.

The window was just big enough for her to squeeze through. She did so carefully, making sure she had a firm grip before letting her legs dangle. She hung that way for a moment. She did not know why, but she couldn't help herself.

You're scared shitless, kid, she told herself.

She looked down. She would be landing in hip-length elephant grass growing wild right up to the base of the back wall of the warehouse. The ground down there sloped away from the building slightly.

She released her grip on the window frame and plummeted. She tried to keep her body loose-limbed for the impact. When she landed, the grass was wet from the misting rain, and she slid down the slope, rolling several times. When she stopped she felt only a slight soreness at her hip where she had first touched the ground.

She stood, whipping her eyes this way and that. She was still not wholly convinced that the unlocked window was not some scheme of Captain Quang's.

The storage building, like a shabby rectangular box with a roof, was shrouded in the mist.

She turned to flee, then stumbled and fell. She picked herself up and continued running.

She expected at any moment that she would hear a shot or a barked command to halt. Of course, if that happened, she would keep on running.

She must get to the base. She must warn them. She must warn Scott!

O God, don't let them catch me! her frenzied mind screamed.

She ran into the jungle.

Captain Quang gathered the people of Vien's unit together at the foot of the ladder to the loft.

"It is time," he told them. "Vien, take your people outside and prepare to leave. We are close to the tunnel."

Vien frowned. "I thought the attack was to take place in the early hours of the morning, after midnight."

"We are going to upscale the attack," said Quang. "We will pour from the tunnel with our weapons blazing. We will toss the explosives, not plant them."

"But the plan was to slip in under cover of darkness. We

were to plant explosives at key points and use force only if our presence was detected."

Vien was aware that the six men and two women of his unit were paying close attention to this exchange. They were loaded down with spare ammo clips, grenades, and pouches containing plastic explosives and detonators. The group radiated an aura of tense anticipation.

"I have changed the plan," Quang said. "Our objective will be pyschological as well as one of attrition. We will not only kill many of them, but every American in Vietnam will know he is not safe from the Vietcong. Do you doubt that I am in command here?"

Vien braced himself against his own uncertainty. "I only ask why, Captain."

"There will be more Americans about. We will kill more of them." Quang stared at the assembled group. "Is there anyone here who is not willing to die for their country?"

As one, the group shook their heads.

"Very well, then," said Quang. "I repeat, Vien. Take your people to the far end of the building outside and prepare to move out."

"What about you, sir?"

"I will see to our prisoner." Quang started up the ladder.

Vien turned to his people. "You heard the captain. Let's go. I hope you are ready. If not, you can run for it. No one will think the less of you for doing so."

"We fight for our country," one of the young women said. We do not run like dogs from our duty."

The others nodded in agreement.

Vien started with them toward the far end of the warehouse. He knew Quang's plan.

Quang intended to use some sort of torture to make the woman prisoner talk, make her tell him where Scott Gaines could be found. Then Quang would slit her throat and re-join them down here to leave for the tunnel.

Quang's roar when he discovered the American missing resounded from the rafters of the dilapidated structure like the howling of a wounded bull.

"Vien, get up here immediately!"

Vien had no choice.

It had been most risky, what he had done. He had gone up the stairs while Quang had napped. He had unlocked the window, shaken the woman awake, and climbed back downstairs. The sentry posted at the foot of the stairs had never suspected a thing.

Quang stood next to the open window. "Well, Vien, explain yourself. What do you know about this?"

Vien had prepared his reply. "I know nothing about this."

"How could she have escaped? You sympathized with her. You set her free while I slept."

"I climbed the ladder once to check on her. She was still unconscious. That was all."

Quang's steady, steely gaze indicated he knew Vien was lying. But he said nothing.

He stormed past Vien and went down the ladder.

Vien went down too. When he joined the group at the far end of the building, Quang was already issuing curt orders.

"You three, go in that direction." He motioned with his arm toward the jungle line visible from the doorway. "You three, spread out and search in the other direction." He addressed the last pair of Vien's teammates. "You two will remain here. Search every inch of ground nearby. We will meet back here in precisely fifteen minutes."

When the others had gone, Vien spoke.

"What would you like me to do, Captain?"

"After our session with the American," said Quang, "you and I went back downstairs and I allowed myself to fall asleep on the floor here. I suppose it was a culmination of things, the heat and the like, but there it is. I fell asleep. And you took advantage of that, didn't you, Vien?"

"I don't know what you're talking about, Captain Quang, I assure you."

Quang unholstered his pistol. "I am sick of your lies, traitor."

"This is why you sent the others away," said Vien. "To kill me."

"And to bring back the woman," said Quang, "though it does not really matter. It will take her time to get her bearings. By then we will already have struck at the base. She will be too late to warn them." His steely eyes glinted with enraged hatred. "You think I'm mad, don't you, Vien?"

"Yes, Captain, you are mad, and so is your plan to send my friends to certain death. It is as if you want to die."

"Quite perceptive, Vien. But then, you are a most intelligent young man. Your problem is that you do not understand that there is no place for compassion in warfare. I am afraid you may be right. I may be mad, but I do not think it matters to this conversation, which will be your last."

"It matters to my friends," said Vien with a nod to the doorway through which his unit had just passed. "They would follow me anywhere. They joined this mission because your son Tsing and I were friends and Tsing enlisted my help in his plans to sabotage the base. When I brought my friends here, I thought we were to undertake that same mission with you."

"Your friends will follow me," said Quang. "You are quite right, Vien. I am mad. There is nothing left for me in life, you see, and that is what will drive a man mad. I expect to die within the next half hour. I welcome death. I will at last be reunited with my wife and children, and my death will be a valiant one, fighting the enemies of our country."

"You take advantage of those willing to die for their beliefs," said Vien. "You want to sacrifice your son's plans and the lives of my friends to your mad dreams of vengeance. And now you will kill me to keep me from swaying them to my way of thinking."

"I will kill you because you are a traitor," Quang snapped.

Vien could tell Quang was about to squeeze the trigger. He leaped—directly at Quang.

They went down together, struggling side by side. The gun left Quang's grip and skittered across the floor.

Quang was the stronger and the more experienced fighter. He brought a knee up into Vien's vital organs, which caused the younger man to loosen the grip he had around Quang's throat. Quang threw himself atop the younger man and unsheathed his combat knife.

With a breathy snarl, Quang leaned forward and rammed the blade of the knife between Vien's ribs.

Vien's body bent into the shape of a bow, and he emitted a gurgling gasp. Blood welled from the wound when Quang extracted the blade.

Quang plunged the blade in a second time.

Vien's body relaxed and his breath escaped with a strangled wheeze. There was a single violent tremor and no more sign of life from Vien.

Quang extracted the knife, cleaned the blade on Vien's shirt. He glanced to the left, to the right.

The warehouse was deserted.

No one had witnessed the killing.

He slid the knife back into its scabbard. Working quickly, he grabbed Vien's body by both ankles and dragged it across the floor to an office area behind a partition.

He stood over the body. "Nothing will stop me from the vengeance I seek." Quang spoke the words to himself like a litany. "I will find Gaines tonight. My son will be avenged and I will be with my family again." He spat down on the body sprawled at his feet.

He returned to the scene of the struggle.

There was a splotch of blood where Vien had fallen. A trail of blood led back to behind the partition.

Quang walked briskly out the doorway. Vien's team were gathered a short distance from the warehouse and were advancing toward it. The misting rain had already soaked them to the skin.

Quang intercepted them.

I have sent Vien for reinforcements."

"When will we strike, Captain Quang?" asked the nearest member of the group, one of the young women.

"We leave to strike now." Quang clipped his words and spoke authoritatively. "Vien and the others will arrive soon enough to do their part."

"We are ready to do our part," said another of the students. "We will follow you, Captain Quang."

"Then let us be gone," said Quang in a quiet voice. "It is time."

Ann could not run. The jungle was too thick for that, the ground too slippery.

Her movement felt more like swimming as she tried to keep her balance through the rapidly gathering gloom of approaching night.

She was running for her life and the lives of American soldiers that would be lost if she did not reach the base at Lai Khe in time.

But she had absolutely no idea where she was. She had lost her bearings when, after the massacre, the bandits had clubbed her unconscious.

She tried to stay calm. It wasn't easy.

She was glad she'd gotten that fitful nap in the loft of the warehouse. It had recharged her, renewed her spirit.

She stopped where she was. The full extent of her plight was suddenly sinking in. Complete darkness was no more than minutes away.

A rubber plantation, she thought. *There has to be a road nearby. I have to cut back toward the warehouse. I'm heading in the wrong direction. . . .*

She started to turn when she caught sight of shifting images coming her way through the shroud of darkening mist. . . .

. . . and plowed straight into another form with enough force to knock the wind from her.

Strong male arms helped her maintain her footing on the slick jungle loam.

Scott Gaines's voice was close to her ear.

"Easy, Ann, easy. You're among friends."

NINETEEN

"Scott! Thank God!"

She plastered herself against him, hugging him to her as if he were as precious as life itself.

The other forms she had seen drew closer.

Hidalgo and DeLuca, like Gaines, wore ponchos against the misting rain. In a moment they were standing to either side of her and Gaines.

She held on to Gaines.

"Thank God," she said again, the words tumbling from her as she felt herself losing control. "Oh, I was praying you'd make it, Scott. They had me. It was Captain Quang, Scott. He's alive."

"We know he's alive, Ann. We know all about it. We've been looking for you, kid. Can you lead us to him?"

She released him then, and pulled back a step.

"I'll take you back," she said. "It's not far."

Tu materialized from where he had been circling the

group. "We are very close to the rubber plantation." He pointed. "That way."

"Yes, that would be it," said Ann. "A storehouse of some kind."

"Thought that damn place was deserted," said DeLuca. "Hell, we've been over that place often enough looking for tunnels to blow."

"I didn't see any digging going on," said Ann. "I got the feeling they were just using it as a place to meet. They're heavily armed."

"We'll stop 'em," said Hidalgo. "The base has stepped up security, the security patrols around the perimeter have been beefed up, and every Tunnel Rat team is combing the terrain. We'll stop them."

"If we're lucky," said Gaines. "Take us there, Ann. It's up to us to shut him down."

A short time later, they crouched just inside the jungle treeline.

The storage house was a ghostly, age-worn presence beyond the curtain of mist and gloom.

"Doesn't feel right," said DeLuca.

"They wouldn't have taken off without leaving someone behind to watch their stuff unless they weren't planning on coming back," said Hidalgo.

"If that's the case," said Gaines, "we've got less time than we thought."

"What do we do, Lieutenant?"

"Cover me," said Gaines. "I'm going in to take a look around."

He advanced at a dodging run toward the warehouse.

Upon reaching the structure, he flattened himself against an outside wall. Then he pulled his M-16 close to his side and propelled himself into the interior of the storehouse, landing in a somersaulting roll beneath any possible line of fire.

There was no gunfire.

Gaines came to his feet and turned slowly in a full circle, his carbine seeking targets.

The interior of the warehouse was shadowy, practically dark. A loft extended over one half of a single wide storage room. There was a partition designed to wall off an office area to his right.

A faint sound came from behind the partition.

A human sound. The sound of man makes when he's dying but there's nothing he can do but hurt and bleed.

Gaines pressed himself against the partition and listened a few moments more. He took a careful look around the partition, fully prepared to open fire.

When he saw a man in VC garb lying there, he pushed away from the wall and returned to the doorway. He waved for the others to join him, then returned to the dying man and knelt beside him.

The man had been stabbed. A thickening puddle of blood on the floor indicated that he did not have long to live.

"Quang," Gaines snapped at the dying man.

Gaines was surprised when the man, appearing to summon up every bit of his fading strength, pointed an extended index finger toward a door in the far end of the storage area.

Tu and Ann Bradley had come in. DeLuca and Hidalgo kept watch outside.

Gaines leaned forward and placed an ear near to the dying man's trembling lips.

"Lai ... Khe ... attack ... tunnel ... north ... perimeter ... Captain Quang ..." were the man's last words.

"He's the one who set me free," said Ann in a small voice. She turned from looking at the corpse. "I don't understand. . . . Why did he do it?"

"Some men are all good and some are all bad, but not many," said Gaines. "But there's no time for that now. We're less than a quarter of a klick from the base right now, and this guy told me the approximate location. Quang's attack is going unless we can short-circuit it."

Tu grabbed for the radio he carried. "I will contact the base."

"Tell them to search inside the north perimeter," said Gaines. "Tell them to draw in the other teams toward the outside of the perimeter, beyond the killing ground. That's where Quang will have his tunnel. Tell them to fire some flares. That should help."

"What about you?" Ann asked.

Gaines started away from her, toward the nearest doorway, beyond which he spotted Hidalgo waiting.

"We're closest to where Quang was heading," he said over his shoulder. "We can get there before the others if we haul ass. It's time Quang and I had it out anyway."

Tu said, "I will come with you."

Gaines paused in the doorway to look back. "No. Ann's been through enough hell for a lifetime today. Get some transportation out here to take you back to the base and stay with Ann until they get here."

"Yes, Sergeant." Tu began speaking into the radio.

Before Gaines could continue out the door, Ann ran to him, threw her arms around him, and hugged him with all her might just long enough to say, "Good luck, soldier."

He returned the hug and said, "Stay strong, Annie. It's almost over." Then he headed out into the rain and the gathering darkness.

Ann stood in the doorway and watched him meet up with Hidalgo and DeLuca, before stalking off.

Annie.

He had never called her that before. No one in the Army had ever called her that before. She liked the way it sounded when Scott Gaines said it.

"Be careful, Scott."

She said it to the darkness, to the rain, to the direction Gaines and his men had taken.

Tu finished speaking into the radio. He stepped over to stand beside her. He, too, stared off into the darkness, into the rain.

"I want very much to go with them," he said.

She nodded. "I know. I know what you mean."

Quang and the eight people of his group reached the ridge above the dip in the terrain where the mouth of the tunnel was concealed.

Complete darkness claimed the wet jungle night. The mist had become a steady downpour.

Quang's son had seen to it that the people who would participate in this night's action had visited this site at some time during the past week in order to memorize the terrain and the placement of the tunnel entrance. Tsing had also briefed each member on their placement and role in the attack. Except for speeding up the timing of the attack, Quang had not variated at all from Tsing's plan.

"Lookouts," said Quang. "Take your positions."

It was impossible to tell that there was a huge military facility so close by. The rolling and climbing terrain blocked it from view even this close beyond the killing ground that the Americans had hacked out of the jungle. The sounds of the base were muted by the steady pouring of the rain.

Quang allowed the lookouts about a half minute to gain their positions: three points of concealment where they could fire upon anyone coming upon the tunnel while the action was in progress.

Lightning seared the night.

In the strobelike lighting, Quang could not see the lookouts.

"Good work, my son," he said under his breath.

Then, in a slightly louder voice so that the remaining five crouched with him could hear, he said, "It is time. Come with me."

They left the ridge, slipping and sliding on uncertain footing down the slight fall in the terrain until they were grouped around the tunnel entrance.

Again carrying out their prearranged instructions, three of the men covered the jungle night with their AK-47s while the remaining two dug away in the pitch blackness, revealing by touch the tunnel entrance.

Then came a *boom!* from the direction of the base, followed by a *whooosh!*

A flare climbed straight up into the night sky with a harsh silvery glare, revealing Quang and the men about to enter the tunnel in stark illumination.

The flare was burning out as it fell back to earth in the near distance.

Gaines, DeLuca, and Hidalgo gained the slippery ridge of the slope in the terrain. A black splotch in the gloom could have been a tunnel entrance, but Gaines could not be sure.

Another *boom! whoosh!* from the direction of the base. Another flare arced into the night sky, casting the area again in a flickering, strobelike brightness.

"There she is," said DeLuca.

Gaines and Hidalgo saw it too. And Gaines saw something else—human forms.

The forms were tracking rifles on them.

"Hit it!" Gaines shouted. "Three of 'em!"

They bellied forward into the muck, tracking their own weapons in the direction of the three figures.

Hidalgo snarled a curse in Spanish.

Then all hell erupted.

The men of Gaines's unit picked their targets without consulting each other in the uncontrollable fury of the moment, but it was a perfectly executed use of firepower.

Gaines took the one on their left. The figure tumbled to the ground, the rifle flying from dead hands.

Hidalgo's rifle jammed. He swore again. He unsheathed his knife and crawled like a slithering snake across the short distance toward the gunner in the middle.

The gunner was so busy firing that he did not see Hidalgo coming until it was too late. Hidalgo came off the ground from beneath the AK-47 and hit the slim figure of the VC. They went back together, and Hidalgo did not waste any time using the combat knife expertly on a couple of vital places.

The gunner went limp.

Hidalgo sat up. The rain slapped his poncho, his face, the blade of the knife, washing it of the fresh blood of this kill.

He turned the corpse over. A girl. A teenage girl. Her head rested so she was looking up at him with eyes that did not blink.

Accusing eyes.

Dead eyes.

Stop it, Hidalgo told himself. Get to work.

He made it over to where Gaines and DeLuca were conferring at the tunnel entrance.

"It's happening," said Gaines. "They'll be coming up inside the base any second."

"Let's hope the guys on the other end do their job," said Hidalgo.

"Let's do our job on this end," DeLuca snarled. "This tunnel is hot. Just the way we like 'em."

"Let's rock and roll." Gaines nodded grimly.

That was all DeLuca wanted to hear. He was the first one of the team to dive into the muddy hole of the tunnel entrance and disappear from sight.

TWENTY

The exchange of gunfire somewhere beyond the northern perimeter drew the attention of every soldier assigned to cover this area.

The base was on full combat alert, men and equipment hurrying everywhere he looked.

Carter left a junior officer in charge of the bunker. He had not been able to remain idly by in the Intel bunker while good men were putting their lives on the line all across the base at Lai Khe. He grabbed his M-16 and stormed out.

Troops had been heavily deployed along the northern perimeter, where Gaines's Kit Carson scout had reported the tunnel exit would most likely be located.

Damn Vietcong, thought Carter. You secure an area, your backyard is more or less secured, and then charlie digs a goddamn tunnel right into it.

Carter had requested that Major Van Dow of the ARVN detachment be apprehended for questioning. The ARVN

MPs were complying without delay for a change.

If Van Dow had assisted the VC in placing the tunnel, he could already be long gone, having slipped off the base in the fear that suspicion would fall on him.

Without quite knowing why, Carter swung around, bringing his rifle on a pair of VC just as the attackers burst from the corner of one of the command bunkers of the ARVN detachment.

Major Van Dow's bunker!

Of course, thought Carter. Final confirmation of what he had not wanted to believe. Major Van Dow was guilty.

The VC swept their fire in wide arcs. They charged screaming from the tunnel, firing as they ran. They did not see Carter.

He triggered a concentrated burst of his own that popped the VC into running, exploding, lifeless scarecrows that crumpled to the muddy earth.

By this time a number of soldiers nearby had identified the source of the attack. When the face of another VC showed itself, it was met with a fiery salvo of rifle and pistol shots that collapsed the tunnel entrance partially.

Carter and everyone else left their positions, advancing on the tunnel on the run.

The attack had been canceled on this end, Carter told himself. Captain Quang's VC had lost their stomach for a real fight.

They were being driven back out through the tunnel.

Straight into the arms of the Tunnel Rats.

The tunnel had been made larger than usual so the attackers could carry their rifles with them. This also made the tunnel easier to navigate for Hidalgo and DeLuca.

They had left their rifles behind. They intended to do their fighting inside this tunnel, unlike the VC they were after. Experience had taught these two Tunnel Rats that mobility was the key to survival.

Each man had his pistol and a flashlight. They held the flashlights away from them to either side to fully illuminate the tunnel ahead. They had thrown off their ponchos before entering the tunnel, which further aided their mobility.

In a squatting crouch, they advanced as quickly as possible, watching every inch of the ground they were covering for booby traps.

Hidalgo wished they could make better time. As he moved along, he used a sleeve to wipe away some of the earth and sweat that filled his eyes.

The face of the young VC woman he'd knifed to death haunted him.

About one hundred feet ahead, the tunnel began curving to the left.

"Here they come," whispered DeLuca, pulling up.

A shuffling and scuffling from around the bend in the tunnel ahead preceded by scant seconds the appearance of two men in VC black pajamas. Each aimed an assault rifle straight ahead at the Americans.

The Americans had had no choice but to hold their fire to prevent mowing down some overenthusiastic grunts from the base. But by the time identification was certain, the VC were already squeezing off one-shot rounds from their rifles.

Hidalgo and DeLuca were on the tunnel floor when the first rounds went over their heads. They had discarded the flashlights, and were using their elbows and both hands to steady their aim as they returned fire.

Each American fired one shot.

The thunder of the assault rifles in the tunnel ceased, and the VC crumpled.

Coughing from the acrid smoke, Hidalgo felt around

and retrieved one of the flashlights. Holding it away from his body, he flicked it on and shone it across the scene in front of the bend in the tunnel.

The smoke and dust curling around the fallen bodies was thicker than fog, but through it could be seen the frightened face of a third VC that had poked itself around the bend.

The face disappeared.

Hidalgo grinned. "Well, all fucking right."

He unsheathed his combat knife, holstered his pistol, and went after the VC, climbing over the corpses like a scuttling crab.

A moment later a high-pitched shriek filled the tunnel, then was abruptly cut short.

DeLuca returned, sheathing the knife.

"You're enjoying this too much, Frank," said Hidalgo.

"Shit on that," snarled Deluca. "Let's see what's up with the lieutenant."

"Must have been mighty important for the lieutenant not to want a piece of this," said Hidalgo.

He decided to worry about DeLuca later. Right now they had to get topside and fast.

They twisted around and started their squatting, crouching withdrawal back the way they had come.

"I see Dow!" Gaines had called into the tunnel after De-Luca and Hidalgo a few minutes earlier. "I'm going after him!"

He could not tell if his men heard him because of a clap of thunder. The thunder seemed to shut off the rain like an automatic switch.

The flare overhead began falling, sputtering out, but its light had been enough for Gaines to positively identify Van Dow.

Gaines was about to enter the tunnel when he saw movement, a figure running away.

The running man slipped, caught himself with both hands to break his fall, and kept on with a look flung back over his shoulder. That's when Gaines IDed him as Dow, the ARVN officer.

He shoulder-slung his rifle and took off at full steam after Dow. He took Dow down with an old-fashioned football tackle to the knees before Dow reached the jungle line of the clearing around the tunnel.

He jumped off Dow, unholstered his pistol, and used his other hand to throw Dow over onto his back. He yanked Dow to his feet.

"Now, Major, do you want to come along to the base quietly, or do I have to persuade you? Go ahead. Don't cooperate. I think I'd enjoy it."

"What . . . what can you mean?" Dow managed in a voice that shook a little. "I did not see that it was you, Lieutenant Gaines." Dow tried a weak smile, but it only made him look sick. "I was coming back to the base. I don't know what happened. I was rushing to report what I saw. Is the base under attack?"

"Can it, shitbag. You were here because you're Quang's top mole inside our ranks. Xong worked under you, like we suspected. We just didn't have the proof. Xong had to be able to move freely to get word back and forth between you and Quang. Xong could not move as freely as he did without your full knowledge."

"But it was I who first reported that Captain Quang was alive after the raid on his tunnel," Dow protested. "I am the one who killed Xong. I am not a spy!"

"You got us word that Quang was alive only because you knew we'd find out sooner or later and you wanted to cover your own ass. You popped Xong to keep him from falling into our hands. You knew he'd break and point the finger at you. You were also good enough to have wounded him if you'd wanted to. I told you we wanted him alive. And now I've got you alive, shitbag, and when we get back to the base, you're the one who's going to break. You can't be the only man Quang has planted in high positions, but I'll bet you know who the others are."

"I will tell you nothing."

"Yes, you will shitbag. And you'll tell us where Quang is. Now start walking while you still can."

A funny look came into Dow's eyes then.

In the light of a new flare fired into the sky, Gaines saw the expression and realized Dow saw something.

A rifle touched the small of Gaines's back.

"I am right behind you, Lieutenant," said Ngai Quang. "You will drop your weapon and move to stand next to Major Dow."

Gaines did as he was told.

Dow realized Quang's rifle was aimed at him and the American together.

"I'm so glad to see you, Captain Quang. I thought you were in the tunnel."

"I would have been had the Americans not ignited the sky with their flare," said Quang. He spoke in English. "At the last minute before entering the tunnel with my men, I saw that all truly was useless. My son's plans and hard work had come to nothing. The Americans knew of the attack. We would be killed as we came out of the tunnel." His glaring eyes focused on Gaines. "I could not go to join my ancestors until I had settled my vengeance with you, Lieutenant Gaines. I knew you were behind this, that you were responsible for the unraveling of this mission. And now is the time of reckoning. You are about to die, Lieutenant. I shall have my vengeance."

"Captain Quang, what about me?" asked Dow.

"You?" Gaines sneered at the man next to him. "You're buying the farm too, shitbag." *Keep this thing in play just a little longer,* Gaines told himself. *Play for time.* DeLuca and Hidalgo might decide to backtrack and check up on him. He kept his eyes on Quang and the AK-47, but he spoke to Dow. "He's going to grease you for the same reason you greased Xong. Kind of poetic, ain't it, Major? Sort of like when you greased your man Xong."

Dow looked to Quang with rising panic. He took one step forward, raising his hands imploringly.

"Captain Quang, *no*! I have been loyal—"

Quang squeezed off a round that blew apart Dow's middle. Then he swung the rifle on Gaines.

Gaines was oddly aware of the peculiar silence of the jungle after the rain. The animal sounds had not yet returned. The rainwater dripping from countless leaves and fronds and vines made a steady splashing sound.

"It is, as you Americans say, payback time, Lieutenant Gaines," Quang said in a sinister voice.

Gaines took one last look at the tunnel in the fading light of the latest flare.

No sign of anyone.

He started to launch himself in a wild sideways dive to at least make a last grasp at life.

The powerful blamming of weapons somehow came sooner than he thought it would, and he heard himself emit a grunt of expelled tension and expectation. But he hit the ground and could still feel, hear, see, and there was no pain.

He came out of a roll, keeping low and springy, fully expecting to find that Quang had somehow missed and was in the process of pulling down on his rifle for another shot.

Instead, Gaines came up just in time to see Quang pitch

forward across the ground, the back of his head and much of his upper back pulped into what looked like shiny black jelly in the flare light.

Quang landed facedown, plastered against the ground next to the tunnel, his lifeblood flowing and dissolving across the mud of the tunnel entrance.

Hidalgo and DeLuca emerged from the tunnel holding pistols. They straightened, glanced around and saw Gaines, and started over.

Gaines was puzzled. What the hell? he wondered. One of those pieces that had downed Quang had been a rifle.

Just then Bok Van Tu emerged from hiding, holding his M-16. Ann Bradley stood next to him, one arm held down at her side holding Tu's pistol.

Gaines grinned. He couldn't help it. It was part admiration of Ann Bradley's true spirit—the lady was a fighter and a winner, no damn mistake—and mostly it was the grin of a man damn glad and lucky to be alive.

"Thought I told you two to stay back at the rubber plantation until reinforcements showed up."

"We thought maybe the reinforcements wouldn't get here in time," said Ann. "Like Captain Quang said, it was payback time."

"I tried to make her stay," Tu said to Gaines. "I am no good at making a woman follow orders."

"Don't feel bad, Tu," said Gaines. "No man is. Thanks, both of you."

The area was coming alive. Choppers hovered in, with spotlights throwing the area into sharp relief, filling the air with their throbbing rotor noises. Troopers were pouring in from every direction at once, on foot and in armored personnel carriers, to secure the area.

No one tried to stop Scott Gaines and his Tunnel Rats

and Ann Bradley as they turned to trudge the short distance back to the base.

Thunder grumbled in the night sky. Or it could have been the pounding of heavy artillery in the distance.

It started to rain again.